PURSUIT

A NOVEL

JAMES KAINE

HORROR HOUSE PUBLISHING

The characters and events portrayed in this book are fictitious. Any similarity to real persons, living or dead, is coincidental and not intended by the author.

ISBNs: 979-8-9867312-0-9 (eBook), 979-8-2180501-8-4 (Paperback), 979-8-9867312-1-6 (Hardcover)

Cover design by: Damonza.com

For Jessica. Thank you for always believing in me. You are my true love and my partner in this life we built together. Without you I would not be able to authentically write about people in love...

...And what I'm about to do to them wouldn't be so horrible.

In loving memory of my father.

I'm sorry I took so long to finish this because now you're not here to read it (which I know you would have, despite the fact that you hated horror fiction). Even so, I know you'd be proud.

I love you and miss you.

Prologue

The Rider could feel the man's panic as he gave chase. The older-model Harley Davidson Chopper mere yards in front of him wobbled as it sputtered under the weight of its operator, moving too fast to maintain any type of consistent stability as the Rider's own beast of a motorbike closed ground. The Rider vaguely recalled that he knew the man, although the picture his clouded memory conjured was notably slimmer and younger, a far cry from the corpulent figure ahead of him who was too rotund to properly manage his ride. He couldn't recall his name. Or how he knew him. He didn't even know why he was rumbling after him on this desolate, wooded road, but he was driven forward by an irresistible need to hunt, despite not knowing what he would do to his prey when he caught him.

He would catch him. There was no doubt about that.

Towering pines bookended the road, offering no hint of civilization on either side, the denizens hidden among thick trunks and dense shrubbery, the shadows of the leaves blanketing the ground. The occasional streetlight mingled with the headlights of the motorcycles as they screamed across the blacktop, but, despite that, visibility was not in large supply. It was the seventeenth year since the cicadas had last invaded the Northeast and they were back with a vengeance. The cacophony of their mating song echoing through the woods, audible even over the roar of American horsepower.

The Rider gripped the hand clutch tight, his black leather gloves hiding the knuckles that practically ripped the rubber from the handle. He was cognizant of an uncontrollable rage growing inside of him with every rotation of his wheel and he knew for the first time since he awoke in the midst of this pursuit that he would kill this man. He would render the flesh from his bones, reveling at the sound as they cracked and tore through his skin. He would crush his skull with his bare hands, feeling his brain matter escape his tensed fingers like an egg yolk.

Why did he feel this murderous urge?

The question was little more than a faint echo in the back of his head. The only thing the Rider cared about was the distance he was rapidly closing on his soon-to-be victim. He could somehow smell the blood pumping from the man's jackhammering heart blowing back with the wind, intertwined with the aroma of a five-dollar handle of whiskey, the kind that comes in a plastic jug and will damn near burn a hole in your esophagus on the way down. He could hear the thumping of the strained organ inside the man's chest and wondered if it would explode before he would catch him. He hoped not. He wanted to be the one to make it stop.

His hatred of this man was thicker than the oppressive humidity of the late-summer air, which was heavy indeed, even at this late hour. His portly prey was surely drenched in sweat from the marriage of strain and stress. The Rider himself was dimly aware of just how hot it was, but it didn't affect him one way or the other. He was beyond that.

The Rider accelerated, his motorcycle moving at a breakneck speed that would surprise any motorcycle aficionado, pushing the vehicle beyond its apparent limits. As he continued to pick up speed, the large man grew even larger in his view. He took note of his leather biker vest—a "cut," they called it—stretched tight over time as the man grew while the garment stayed the same size. He didn't know quite how he was aware of such lingo, even as he himself was expertly operating a motorcycle, but the symbol adorned on his target's back was at once familiar and foreign.

It was a contradiction that didn't matter. He was close now.

The man must have sensed the Rider bearing down on him because he lurched his bike off the road and into a clearing in the trees. He must have been aware that the opening would be there because the Rider doubted the man had the dexterity to pull off such a move blind. Even with the man's awareness, the maneuver was unsuccessful. The Rider braked, skidding to an implausible, burning stop as he watched his opponent's headlight sway as his bike teetered out of control, crashing to the ground with a dull, heavy thud, slamming its occupant to the ground with thunderous force.

He heard the man curse and cough through labored breaths as he dismounted. He listened as his target struggled to his feet before stumbling through the trees. The Rider took his time. He wasn't at all concerned that the man would elude him. His movements were deliberate as he reached toward the worn leather scabbard on the side of his bike. He didn't recall the weapon being there previously, but showed no hesitation in drawing the machete from its sheath, taking a moment to admire the glint of the steel in the moonlight. The blade was old, but still razor sharp, leaving no doubt that it would have little trouble doing its job.

The Rider needed to feel the metal tear through the man's meaty stomach. He yearned to watch as his insides spilled from his torso onto the ground in a steaming puddle of gore. A guttural scream welled inside, aching to project from his lungs, but it did not escape him. It only insulated his body with fury and mania. He clutched the instrument of death in his grip and stepped off the highway, feeling the ground soften under his boots as he entered the woods.

He moved at a steady pace, the large, slow man making more than enough noise for the Rider to track him. The footsteps ahead occasionally decreased in volume, but never fell silent. The Rider was not running, but was distantly aware that he was moving very fast. Faster than one would have thought possible.

He heard the man cough. It was a wet, gurgling sound that betrayed the severity of his injuries. The Rider increased his pace, not wanting his victim to expire before he got his hands on him. It wasn't long before he saw the outline of the man through the trees. His body couldn't match his will and he was clearly slowing, even though his feeble attempt to keep moving forward demonstrated that he wasn't resigned to his fate.

Finally, the man crumpled to the ground, unable to maintain his feet underneath him any longer. He attempted to crawl forward, his fingers clawing into the dirt, an effort he almost immediately found futile. The Rider saw the man finally give up as his body slumped down on his stomach as if he just finished an intense set of push-ups. With his prey immobilized, the Rider slowed his own pace, allowing him to relish the fact that he had this man exactly where he wanted him.

The man lay prone for a few moments before he managed to struggle to his hands and knees. He crawled toward the closest pine like a determined toddler and hugged the branch, trying in vain to pull himself back to his feet. Finding the effort too taxing with his injuries, he instead twisted into a seated position, resting his back against the tree. The Rider stopped in front of him and tilted his head, observing him like an artist admiring his work.

The man looked up at his pursuer, his battered body too tired to be scared any longer. His look was that of someone who fully expected this, but somehow still couldn't believe it. He shook his head in his disbelief and reached into his vest, retrieving a soft pack of unfiltered Camel cigarettes and a shiny lighter emblazoned with the same logo as his vest. The Rider's rage rose again at the sight of the symbol, but he remained motionless. He didn't know what about the imagery offended him so, but looking at it made his blood boil. The man shook the pack, pushing one of the cigarettes through the opening. He parted his cracked lips and grasped the rolled tobacco between yellowed, bloodstained teeth. They were mostly intact. The blood must have been coming up from inside.

"You sure took your sweet ass time," the man said in a gravely voice. "I guess you always were a persistent son of a bitch."

The Rider didn't answer. Didn't know what he would say if he did. Hell, he didn't even know if he could speak at all. So many questions, but none were relevant at this moment. All that mattered was what was about to happen and the euphoria it would bring.

The man flicked the flint wheel a few times before the flame finally emanated from the lighter's eyelet, illuminating the dark bags under his weary eyes as he held it to the tip of the cigarette, sparking it to life. When the puff of smoke confirmed that it was lit, he flicked the lighter closed and attempted to return it to his vest. His shaky hands had other plans, however, as it slipped from his grip and landed in a bed of leaves below. He didn't bother to recover it. They both knew he wouldn't need it anymore. The man took a deep drag from his cigarette. Apparently too deep because he coughed violently. Dark-red blood, the result of internal injuries, sprayed out, matting the hair of his scraggly salt-and-pepper beard. The attack lasted for what felt like ages, but the Rider was not inclined to interrupt it. The man's prolonged suffering was satisfying to watch. Once the episode stopped, the man hesitated but took another drag, a smaller, more tentative one this time, but one that still resulted in another, less intense coughing fit. Undeterred, the man took a third drag that he managed to control better than the previous two, even though it looked like it took a Herculean effort to do so. He blew the smoke at the Rider, a futile gesture of defiance that took way too much effort as it was followed by another heavy, hacking cough.

"So this is it, huh? You think that's gonna make it all better? Your hands are just as dirty as mine. Shit, ain't no one's hands dirtier than yours, motherfucker."

The Rider maintained his silence. The man flicked his cigarette at him, but didn't get enough on it to make the point he wanted. The butt bounced off the Rider's left thigh. He didn't flinch as the embers cascaded off of his pants.

"This shit is on you, asshole! You can blame us all you want, but you're the one! It's your fault that—"

His final sentence remained forever unfinished as the Rider severed his vocal chords with one deft swipe of the machete. His mouth went wide as the blood cascaded down his neck and onto his chest. The Rider stepped forward and grabbed the man's stringy hair, wrenching his head upward and causing the wound to gape, the pristine edges of the cut transitioning into jagged tears as he beheaded the man with his bare hands, the spine snapping and dangling from the stump. He held the man's head up to his eye level. Some people said that a severed head can maintain consciousness for several seconds after removal. The Rider was able to confirm that theory as he watched the man's life expire. The seconds between decapitation and death were indeed scant, but they were long enough for the Rider to savor.

He tossed the head into the dead man's lap and turned back toward the road. When he got back to his bike, he sheathed the weapon, not bothering to clean off the blood. He mounted his ride and started the engine, roaring off into the night without purpose or destination.

At least not for now.

Chapter 1

Ava's eyes fluttered open. She was in a bed, a rather comfortable one at that, but was not immediately aware of where she was or how she got there. She remained on her back while her vision adjusted before sitting up and glancing around at her surroundings. The silk sheets slid down around her waist, the brisk breeze from the air conditioning washing over her naked skin. She glanced to her left, observing that the bed was of the king-size variety, but she was alone, at least in the immediate vicinity. The sound of running water from the bathroom indicated that she wasn't completely solo. As she surveyed her surroundings, she took comfort in the fact that she was exactly where she was supposed to be, although the particulars of how she got there before going to sleep were hazy at best.

She turned over to find the other side of the bed empty. She remembered Jeremy being there when they had fallen asleep, but he was gone now. She deduced that he was clearly the bathroom's current occupant.

She smiled as she held her left hand up to inspect the only things she wore—two rings. The first was an impressive cushion-cut diamond engagement ring set in a white gold band with smaller diamonds adorning the brackets that held the shiny rock in place. The second was a rhodium-plated white gold band with an intricate woven pattern engraved around its radius. She had gotten used to the fit of the diamond, but the wedding band was new enough that she was still aware of its presence even when she wasn't looking at it. But the fit was perfect and she knew soon it would be like a part of her, noticeable only when looking at it.

Ava still couldn't believe she and Jeremy had gone through with it. The "ceremony" was nothing more than a jaunt over to City Hall where filling out the paperwork took longer than the nuptials themselves. At least Loretta, the stern-looking woman behind the window that served as their altar, was kinder than her features had predicted. She'd dutifully recited the vows that brides and grooms parrot back to each other. The words were the typical "do yous?" followed by "I dos." Thinking back on it, Ava would have loved it if they had written their own vows, but they were more concerned with actually becoming husband and wife than how they got there. A big, blustery celebration was not on the docket.

What the wedding itself lacked in pomp and circumstance, they more than made up for during the wedding night. Their honeymoon destination, Atlantic City, was about a two-hour drive, but they made it only about forty-five minutes before pulling over on a back road to consummate their union. Thinking back on it, Ava was sure that more than a couple of passing motorists solved the mystery of the car with the steamed-up windows on the side of the road. At least she and Jeremy were considerate enough to leave the top up. Once they checked in to the hotel, the rest of the evening was a blur of eating, drinking and lovemaking with the kind of stamina that only young newlyweds possess. It was a great night, but the pounding in her temples and the desert in her mouth was the inevitable receipt for their revelry.

The morning sun squeezed through the slit of the drawn blinds, trying its damnedest to light up the room. Ava wasn't in love with the concept of letting the room bathe in sunlight, mainly due to the effect it would probably have on her hangover, but she didn't want to just sit in the dark either. She could just flip on one of the lights, but the window was closer than any of them, so she chose efficiency. She bit the bullet and flipped the covers off herself before standing up, taking a second to stretch before tossing the blinds open. She flinched a bit as the sunlight bathed the room. The sensation of the heat was a nice contrast from the chilly blast of the air conditioning. She always needed to sleep cold, but sometimes it was a bit much when she woke up with her room feeling like winter.

With the blinds open, Ava stifled an urge to giggle as she assessed the state of the room which was, to say the least, in a state of disarray.

Clothes were strewn about like a trail of breadcrumbs leading from the door to the bed. Ava noted that the "Do Not Disturb" door hanger was still on the inside of the room. Oops. That would have been something if housekeeping walked in at any point during their celebration. Although she doubted they would have been the first guests to forget to take precautions to the detriment of the poor hotel staff. Two empty champagne bottles rested next to the dresser. There were no glasses, however, as they'd opted to consume the bubbly booze direct from the bottle in addition to few other decidedly more scandalous places. Overall, it seemed every piece of furniture was displaced, every corner of the room an exhibit solving the case of what had gone on in the newlyweds' hotel room.

As she pondered how to even begin tidying the room up, she became aware of a different ache than the one in her head. This soreness on the left side of her torso. She lightly ran her fingers across the newly etched tattoo in the skin covering her rib cage. It was still covered in clear plastic wrap. She didn't remember exactly what time they had finished at the tattoo parlor, but she thought she recalled the artist telling her to leave it wrapped for twelve to twenty-four hours. By her estimation, it was close enough to at least the lower mark, so she carefully peeled it away to reveal the script inked horizontally in two lines across her skin:

Today is all we have.
Tomorrow isn't guaranteed.

She smiled, recalling the absolute spontaneity of the moment. They had just finished dinner and Ava was joking that they should get tattoos. Neither had any, but Ava, in the spirit of throwing caution to the wind, figured fuck it. She'd wanted to get one for a while, but hadn't thought Jeremy would go for it. Wouldn't want to blemish his pretty skin. But when he said, "Let's do it," she was pleasantly surprised. Her straitlaced hubby rarely stepped outside his comfort zone and she agreed instantly, not wanting to give him a chance to change his mind.

As they left the restaurant, Jeremy typed "tattoo parlors Atlantic City, NJ" into his phone and found two nearby, one on the boardwalk and another in a less desirable part of the city. They opted for the boardwalk, but when their rideshare dropped them off, they found it was closed. Ava figured Jeremy would back out at this point, but he pulled his phone back up and said, "It's only an eight-minute walk. Let's just go for it."

An hour and a half later, they had gotten their ink and were on their way back to the hotel, Ava marveling at Jeremy's rare display of adventurousness. Upon their arrival, they made a beeline for the bar in the center of the casino floor and each did a shot of Southern Comfort and lime—SoCo and lime being the colloquial way to request it. The rest of the night was a blur from there.

Outside the window, the Atlantic Ocean was calmer than usual. Summer was winding down, but enthusiastic beachgoers were set up along the shoreline. As far as Jersey Shore locales went, Atlantic City wasn't a family-friendly resort town like Ocean City or Point Pleasant. It attracted mostly younger people, looking to party. As she observed the throngs on the beach, it occurred to Ava that she didn't even know what time it was, so she glanced at the clock.

11:23 a.m.

She started retrieving the clothing from the floor. Becoming aware that she had still not flipped the "Do Not Disturb" sign to the exterior of the room, she grabbed the nearest garment, a T-shirt with a tuxedo design that Jeremy had worn to City Hall yesterday.

Feeling more modest, Ava popped the sign of the door handle and cracked open the door just enough to slip her arm through. She flipped the sign to "Service Please" and placed it on the outside handle before shutting the door and resuming the task of gathering the garments from the floor, piling them in her arms and flopping them into an open suitcase in the far corner of the room.

As she tossed them in, her dry mouth and achy head were kind enough to remind her of her hangover. No wonder from looking at the champagne bottles. They would have been bad enough on their own, but she didn't need to recall the entire evening to know that they had consumed much more than that. She picked them up using her fingers to wrap around both necks simultaneously and dropped them in the wastebasket near the dresser. As she did, she experienced a new symptom, one that, unlike the others, elicited concern. She suddenly became aware that she was very lightheaded.

She gingerly made her way to one of the chairs bookending a circular table in front of the window and braced herself as she lowered herself down into the seat. She placed her head between her hands and started slowly and firmly rubbing her temples. She mouthed a silent plea to God that the episode wouldn't linger. The last thing she wanted the day after her wedding was a trip to the emergency room.

She was so focused on willing her dizziness away, she didn't hear the shower stop. Or the bathroom door open. She only became aware of it once Jeremy's voice broke her trance.

"Hey there!"

She looked up at him, hoping he wouldn't notice her glassy eyes or, if he did, that he would simply attribute it to the hangover. The sight of her new husband was almost enough to make her forget how awful she felt in that moment. He was wearing only a fluffy white towel embroidered with the casino logo wrapped around his waist. He stood just a hair under six feet tall and his well-sculpted chest and ab muscles still glistened from the shower. He also sported a new tattoo, deliberately placed on his left pectoral over his heart. It had an oily sheen to it. To no one's surprise, Mr. Responsible over there had already applied the ointment as instructed. The ink was the same script as Ava's, but his read:

Ava Allegretti
08-24-22
Forever & Always

Ava had asked him why he used her maiden name, especially since she had told him that she had every intention of taking his name, even though it'd likely be months before she actually got around to the actual paperwork. He simply told her, "I fell in love with Ava Allegretti and on August 24, 2022, I married her," before jokingly confirming her penchant for procrastination, "And knowing you, we'll be in our sixties before you actually fill out the name change forms."

Ava tried not to adversely react to her husband's quip. She knew he certainly didn't intend to hit this old, exposed nerve, but by the look on his face, he knew he had. Ava wondered if the realization was borne out of self-recognition or her failure to hide her expression. Ava was never the best at that. She knew girls who had "resting bitch face," but Jeremy coined his own term for Ava: "active bitch face." If she was annoyed or pissed off, she couldn't hide it if she tried. Which she typically didn't.

His hair, usually parted and slicked, hung down loosely in front of his eyes. He pushed it back out of his sight line, revealing his baby blues, which were full of concern.

"What's wrong?" he asked.

"I'm fine," she replied, hoping she was effectively playing it off. "Just one too many last night."

She could tell Jeremy wasn't convinced, but he offered her a smile and his hands, which she accepted as he helped her out of the chair and embraced her. His skin felt incredible against her, even through the cloth of the T-shirt. She could happily stay like this for hours. As she nestled her head against Jeremy's chest, he whispered to her.

"You sure there's nothing you're not telling me?"

She tilted her head back and saw the worry in her spouse's demeanor. Fortunately, the dizziness had finally started to pass. With her own fears assuaged, she could offer a more convincing reassurance. "I'm *fine*," she said punctuating the sentence with a kiss. "Stop being such a worry wart."

"Worry wart? You sound like my grandmother."

She pushed him backward. He was too close to the bed and ended up falling back on the mattress, which was far too soft to cause any kind of physical harm, although it did cause the knot in his towel to loosen. Ava frowned and put her hands on her hips, giving him a bemused look as she pulled her shirt up and off, tossing it to the side of the bed, inadvertently draping it over the lamp.

"You can look at me like this and think of your grandmother?"

"Some guys think of baseball."

"Oh, really?" she said chucking the shirt at him. "If that's what you're thinking of when you look at me, you ain't getting in this dugout anytime soon."

Jeremy smirked and pulled her down onto the bed with him, rolling on top of her and completely losing his towel in the process. Ava suddenly remembered that she had put the door hanger outside requesting maid service. Oh, well, housekeeping would probably knock before coming in.

Probably. She looked down at Jeremy and cocked an eyebrow at him.

"What are you waiting for? Is it time for the second-inning stretch?"

"You mean the seventh-inning stretch."

"Shut the fuck up. You know I prefer football."

She silenced him with a kiss. Then another. And another. She reached down and wrapped her fingers around his erection, stroking it as she guided him into her. Playfulness gave way to passion and, within moments, their worries were gone.

At least for now.

An hour later, the weary, dehydrated couple made their way downstairs to get something to eat. At this point it was almost one in the afternoon, so they opted to head for the pool bar. This particular hotel was well known for its indoor pool that morphed into a nightclub once the sun went down. It was one of the hottest spots in town, but not just anybody could get in. Fortunately, Jeremy had a high-level player's card, so not only did they get in, they didn't have to pay the exorbitant cover charges, even for lunch. Ava was never one to put any type of emphasis on money or material things. She grew up poor, the daughter of immigrants who fought and scratched for everything they had. Basically, the exact opposite of Jeremy who came from money. She didn't know him when they were teenagers, but he told her he never had to worry about where his next meal was coming from and always had the newest, most fashionable clothes for school.

That's not to say that Jeremy was ignorant of the dichotomy. In fact, his awareness and acknowledgment of the differences in their upbringings was one of the many things Ava loved about him. She recalled the first time he met her parents. Her parents insisted on taking them out to dinner and, although Jeremy could have gotten a reservation for any restaurant in town based on his name alone, he happily accepted the invite to a nice BYOB Italian place with mid-level pricing and red-and-white checkered tablecloths. He made a point to rave about how good the food was, making sure Mama and Papa Allegretti felt appreciated. When the check came, he politely offered to pay for their share, but was not so insistent as to put up a fight when Papa insisted that the meal was on him and that there would be no further discussion on the matter.

Jeremy learned a lot about his future in-laws that evening. Giuseppe Allegretti's parents were part of a large influx of Italian immigration to Argentina shortly after the end of World War II. Giuseppe, or Joe, as he started to go by when he came to America, was born and raised in Argentina in the 1960s and met Martina Montero when he was in his twenties. Shortly after they got married in the late 1980s, they sold a small piece of land they inherited from his father's family in Italy and used the money to come to America. Ava was born almost ten years later. One of the biggest questions she always got was how she ended up with the name Ava which isn't traditionally Italian or Argentinian. The answer was relatively simple. Her mother's favorite movie was *The Barefoot Contessa* and she insisted on naming her after Ava Gardner. Joe had preferred Valentina, which was his grandmother's name, but when Martina got insistent on a topic, she was rarely swayed: "I took your last name, so now I name the baby."

During that dinner, Joe told many stories in his endearing broken English—as was his MO—especially about how he had worked as a handyman when he first came to America, before he and Martina had saved enough to open up a small deli which had somehow managed to survive and thrive by offering fresh, high quality food representing the best of the Allegretti's combined cultures, something the big chain supermarkets just couldn't compete with. Papa credited most of their modest success to frugal living, smart investing and service with a human touch that the bigger stores lacked. Their customer base was small, but loyal. Ava had heard most of the tales of his handyman days ad nauseam, especially the ones of his more colorful clientele, such as the guy who wanted his lawn cut on the lowest setting despite repeated warnings about sun damage; the couple who ignored his advice to remove a dying tree branch which subsequently ended up on their Mercedes one particularly windy evening; and—Mama's least favorite—the lady who loved to sunbathe nude.

That was the night Jeremy learned the word *mujerzuela*. Although Mama wouldn't tell him what it meant. Ava translated on the car ride home that it meant *slut*. Jeremy guffawed at such a word coming from Mama Allegretti's mouth.

Jeremy confessed to Papa that he was a tad jealous, not of the exhibitionist sunbathers, but of the idea of working outdoors.

"My dad never let me cut the grass or mess around in the garden, even when I told him I wanted to learn. He told me he wanted it done right, so leave it to the guys he hired."

"He wouldn't let you even try?" Papa asked.

"Nope. He was too concerned with appearance. His clothes, his car, his hair. Even his lawn. He couldn't risk being seen as less than perfect. I used to follow our landscapers and contractors around, asking if I could help. My dad would get completely pissed off and tell me to stop bugging the help."

"Why were you so interested in manual labor? Especially when your family could afford to hire people to do it?"

"The truth is that when I was young, I wanted to draw comic books for a living. I wanted to be the next Jim Lee or Todd McFarlane."

Ava suppressed a grin as Papa nodded like he knew who those guys actually were.

"But my dad always told me that I was never going to make any money doing that. He said I'd never afford a house like the one we lived in, let alone staff to take care of it. So, I figured I'd just have a smaller house and have to cut back on some of the luxuries. That meant I'd have to learn to take care of it myself."

"That's quite admirable for someone so young to think so practically."

Ava had wrapped her arms around Jeremy and pulled herself into him. "That's why we work so well! He keeps me grounded."

"Well, that's certainly a full-time job in itself," Mama chimed in.

Jeremy kissed Ava on the cheek and smiled. "It certainly is," he said. "But she stops me from being so uptight. At least every now and then."

"Do you feel that comes from how you were raised?" Papa asked. Again, without pretense. "Being more measured?"

"I don't want money to be the defining pursuit in my life. I mean, I certainly want to be well-off and able to support a family. When I become a father, I want my children to know that they just can't expect to pay someone to do things for them. I want them to know the value of hard work."

Ava's fondness of the memory dampened a bit as she recalled her parents' faces. Jeremy was never the best at reading a room, bless his heart, so he didn't notice that, upon mention of children, Ava's parents had given her a look that he now understood more or less said to her, "Don't fuck this up."

The topic of children was broached eventually and Ava made her position clear. It wasn't that she didn't want to be a mom, but she felt she couldn't. Jeremy was a trooper of course, being kind and understanding of her concerns on the surface, but she knew deep down that he hoped she would change her mind as their relationship progressed. Even though she made it clear that it wasn't a matter of "want." Her parents didn't help either. She knew they desperately wanted grandchildren, a desire that only intensified as they got to know Jeremy better. They adored him. Her father had later told her that Jeremy asked permission to marry her that night at dinner when she and Mama had excused themselves to use the restroom before they left. Papa had given his blessing, even though they had only been dating a few weeks. Jeremy made it clear that it wasn't going to be right away, but he told Papa that he knew that was what he wanted.

Five months later, he followed through and here they were, married and about to stuff their faces at the hotel pool bar on their honeymoon.

Jeremy pulled a bar stool out for her. Always the gentleman. They sat at the bar and ordered a myriad of appetizers: chicken quesadillas, buffalo wings and loaded nachos, arranged like a volcano erupting with cheese, ground beef, onions and avocado. Greasy food was the best remedy for a hangover. They started out with a couple of waters, making sure to hydrate, but by the time the food came, they performed the requisite mental gymnastics to convince themselves there was no better cure for their condition than the hair of the dog that bit them. Ava got a tequila sunrise, a bold choice to be sure. The visual appeal of the beverage with its orange coloring swirled with red from the grenadine floated on top belied the potency of the base alcohol underneath. Jeremy decided on a Stella Artois, trying to be responsible by selecting the sixteen-ounce glass over the twenty-two. Although that went out the window when he ordered the larger version for his second round.

They ate in silence for a while, reveling in their caloric intake as they had worked up quite a voracious appetite with their shenanigans over the past twenty-four hours. When Jeremy finally needed a breather and pushed his plate away, he asked, "So, what do you want to do today?"

Ava paused long enough to wash down a bite of chicken wing with a sip of her drink. "Let's go lie out on the beach for a little bit, then we can get ready to go out tonight."

"You don't want to just stay in and get room service?"

"Why? It's our honeymoon."

"Yeah, but we pushed it pretty hard last night—"

"What? Can't hang, Mr. Carlisle?"

Jeremy frowned. "One—don't call me that. Two—I'm just saying there's nothing wrong with taking it easy for a night."

"Baby, we're young and just got married and you're over here acting like we're already Carl and Ellie."

Ava realized too late that referencing the beloved couple from the Disney movie, *Up*, probably wasn't the best analogy. Looks like Jeremy wasn't the only one who could put his foot in his mouth. She could see some moisture in the corner of Jeremy's eye and realized she should change the subject, so she leaned in and kissed him.

"Come on, dude, settle up the bill so we can go soak up some sun."

Ava and Jeremy made their way down the boardwalk onto the beach. It was decently crowded, but, being a Sunday, it wasn't intolerable, most likely due to the fact that it was the week before Labor Day and, frankly, the beach was always the secondary attraction in Atlantic City. People mostly came here to gamble and hit the clubs. Ava could feel Jeremy's frown without even looking at him as they stepped onto the sand.

"What?" she asked.

"Nothing."

"Mmm-hmm."

He sighed. "We have to go on a proper honeymoon. Somewhere where the water is blue. Not the lovely 'Jersey green' we have here."

She grabbed his left arm and wrapped her own around his bicep. "Babe, there is nowhere I'd rather be right now! This is our home and I love it! It's got a certain trashy charm that other locales lack."

As if on cue, Jeremy tapped her shoulder and pointed to a discarded condom wrapper by one of the wood pylons. "How delightfully charming," he quipped in an abysmal attempt at a British accent.

They burst into laughter, a little delirious from their lack of sleep. Ava slid her arm down Jeremy's and grabbed his hand, leading him to a spot she'd eyed. "Here! This is perfect!"

They didn't have much with them, just a bag with some towels and two extra-large bottles of water they'd purchased from the gift shop before heading down. They carefully laid the towels out and stripped down to their swimsuits. Jeremy's wrapping on his freshly inked tattoo was starting to peel off, so he smoothed it out carefully, making sure the area was completely covered. Ava went about applying sunscreen to her own, uncovered ink. She felt Jeremy's eyes on her, but tried to ignore him, but with no such luck.

"Don't you think you should cover that up?"

Ava didn't look at him as she continued to work it in. "Nah. It's fine."

"The guy said to avoid direct sunlight."

"I am. I'm putting sunscreen on. Duh."

"You know that's not—"

"Look, bikini season is only a few more weeks. I got this beautiful new tattoo in honor of you, my love, and I want to show it off."

Jeremy shook his head. He had to know he was too rigid a lot of the time and was less than likely to win this argument, but she also knew that once he'd started down this road, he might as well go down swinging. "Is it worth showing off the ink if it's blotchy and red from an infection? Or if you get sepsis from swimming in the ocean?"

Ava rolled her eyes. "Seriously, you worry too much."

Jeremy muttered under his breath. "Someone has to."

Ava caught the remark. "What's that supposed to mean?"

Jeremy looked ahead at the ocean, knees drawn into his chest. He responded without turning to her. "You know what I mean."

"Why don't you explain it to me like I don't?"

Jeremy sighed, but otherwise stayed silent, continuing to stare at the waves that rolled up to the shore, before receding back to the vast expanse.

Ava, however, wasn't about to drop the subject. She answered for him. "You wish I'd take better care of myself."

It came out more bluntly than she intended. Her annoyance at her husband waned as she looked in his eyes, seeing his pain. Jeremy was never one to shy away from showing his emotions, an aspect of his personality that she absolutely adored, but it was maddening when she tried to stay angry at him.

"Babe..." She trailed off, not quite sure how to continue. She long ago made the vow that she would never be held back or restrained by her physical limitations. Her parents had raised their own objections, but over time had learned to accept that Ava was going to do things on her own terms. Jeremy, on the other hand, was stubborn as hell. She didn't want him fussing over her constantly, but at the same time, she didn't want her issues to define her life. This was certain to be the biggest conflict their fledgling matrimony would face. He would sacrifice anything for more time, even if that meant diminished quality. Ava, on the other hand, preferred not to worry about the amount of time, focusing instead on how she used it.

This was not about the tattoo. It never was.

She watched Jeremy remain stone-faced as he stared out over the Atlantic. She didn't like it, but she understood that it came from a place of love. Some compromise had to be in order, no matter how small.

She reached into her bag and located the wrapping she had already known Jeremy had packed, because he knew she wouldn't. She carefully applied it over the tattoo, making sure it was completely covered.

"Better?"

Jeremy still didn't respond, but she noted the tension in his posture, a sure sign that he was actively trying not to look at her, out of sheer obstinance at this point. She smiled and gave him a light shove. He rocked, but didn't fall over. She pushed him again, a little harder this time. The hint of a smile starting to pierce his stony demeanor.

She had him now.

She started rapidly poking his arm, trying to get him to laugh. His smile widened, but he didn't totally break. He finally looked in her direction, no longer able to maintain the veneer of irritation.

"Real mature!"

She gave him the smile. It wasn't her typical smile, but a half-smirk that she gave him, typically in lieu of an apology, when it was time to stop arguing. It worked every time. No matter how mad he thought he was, when she hit him with that grin, it was over. This time was no exception.

Jeremy laughed. "You're a pain in the ass, you know that?"

She threw her arms around him and kissed him hard on the cheek. "But I'm your pain in the ass."

She didn't let him go. Instead he leaned into her. She moved her arm up to stroke his hair. Her sweet, sensitive man. "I love you, baby. I know you only want what's best for us."

Ava gently pulled Jeremy toward her slightly, making sure he was off-balance before abruptly letting him go as she bolted to her feet, the beach towel the only thing preventing him from swallowing a mouthful of sand. She giggled as she took off toward the water.

"Catch me if you can, slowpoke!"

CHAPTER 2

The next morning, the couple woke up in their hotel room, which was once again in disarray with clothing, liquor bottles and a pillaged room service tray, its previous contents unidentifiable as the only remnants were crumbs and a smear of ketchup. They had clearly worked up an appetite with the prior day's activities.

Ava stirred first; the pounding in her head was back, a sensation that was starting to become a little too familiar. She had obviously won the "go out" versus "stay in" argument. It pleased her competitive spirit, even though she was paying for it now. She shook her head as she remembered Papa's words of wisdom when it came to hangovers: "If you want to dance, you have to pay the fiddler."

And this particular fiddler was an expensive one. She chuckled, knowing full well that Joe wouldn't approve of her drinking like this, even though he always maintained a sense of humor about it. She remembered

New Year's Eve when she was fifteen. They had gone to her cousin's house and, of course, the teens had absconded with a rather pricey bottle of vodka while the adults were distracted with their own revelry. It wasn't a lot, but their alcohol tolerance were all but nonexistent. To Papa's credit, he didn't get angry when she threw up in his car on the ride home. He simply tucked her in, kissed her goodnight and promptly woke her up at seven in the morning to go to Home Depot with him to get paint for the kitchen that she would spend the rest of the day painting, stopping occasionally to dry heave after she had expelled the rest of the booze.

It was a good two years before she attempted to drink again.

She looked at Jeremy, still sound asleep on his side, facing away from her. He looked so damn cute to her that she started devising creative ways to wake him up.

That is until the booming sound of flatulence trumpeted from beneath the sheets, the inevitable result of the mixture of booze and 3 a.m. room service. She giggled as she covered her nose, her sleeping beau oblivious to the world.

Perhaps a shower instead.

When she got out of the shower, Jeremy was awake, propped up in bed as he scrolled through his phone, absentminded.

"You check the sheets for stains?"

Jeremy looked up, confused. "Huh?"

Ava laughed. "Never mind. The bathroom's yours if you need it."

Jeremy pondered for a second, placing his hand on his stomach. "Yeah. I should, um, shower."

He hopped out of bed and bounced into the bathroom, shutting the door quickly behind him.

Ava got dressed while Jeremy was in the bathroom. She chose garments geared toward comfort than aesthetics. After two days of newly marital bliss, she knew neither of them would mind. She pulled on an old pair of jean shorts and a gray tank top. She wanted to be as comfortable as possible with the drive back north ahead of them. It had been about ten minutes since Jeremy went into the bathroom, but she just now heard the shower door open, despite what was clearly Jeremy's best efforts to do it slow enough to avoid the creaking sound it would inevitably make. He had started the water and the overhead fan as soon as he entered, the noise a not-so-subtle subterfuge to protect Ava from the less glamorous aspects of marriage.

"Must have been a rough one," she thought to herself, simultaneously amused by and appreciative of the effort.

She gathered up their garments, checking under the bed and table to make sure they hadn't flung any out of sight during their more often than not rapid disrobing over the past forty-eight hours. Satisfied that everything was accounted for, she started piling them in their suitcase, not bothering to fold anything. It was all going right in the washer when they got home. A weekend at the casino all but guaranteed that your clothes would reek of smoke, even if you weren't a tobacco user yourself. It always amazed her how much stronger the smell was when they unpacked at home than in the hotel itself, even in a non-smoking room. She tossed a pair of Jeremy's athletic shorts and his favorite T-shirt on the bed so he had something to change into out of the shower, knowing he'd also want to be as relaxed as possible for the trek home.

As she mashed the clothing down to make enough room to get the suitcase zipped, orchestral music blasted from Jeremy's phone, startling her. She immediately recognized it as the music that played when Darth Vader was on screen in the *Star Wars* movies. It was a tune that was actually more ominous in real life because she knew Jeremy assigned that particular ring tone to someone very specific.

His father.

Ava's good mood dissipated. While her parents were nothing but supportive of the young couple's relationship, to say Jeremy's father disapproved was an understatement. Andrew Carlisle was, simply stated, a dick. He was a dick to Jeremy. He was a dick to Jeremy's mother. He was dick to the two women he married after Jeremy's mother. He was a dick to waiters, bellhops and flight attendants. He was a dick to Ava, although not overtly, a factoid that Ava considered, were he capable of cordial human interaction, might mean he didn't completely hate her. At best, she was a non-entity to him.

Jeremy had held off introducing her to his father for as long as he could; their meeting was delayed until long after Jeremy had met Joe and Martina. His parents had divorced when he was only five years old and his mother, Layla, had received primary custody. Jeremy had said that his dad was supposed to have him every other weekend, but, more often than not, he bailed on those visits, citing work as his excuse. Whenever Layla tried to call Andrew out on it, he just snidely commented about needing the extra hours to cover alimony and child support. That, of course, was bullshit. Andrew was one of the most successful real estate investors in the tri-state area, with an eight-figure net worth. But, as successful as he was at putting together a real estate deal, that was how shitty a dad he was.

Unfortunately for Andrew, shitty or not, he had to become a full-time parent when Layla passed away from ovarian cancer when Jeremy was eight years old. Ava sometimes wondered if it was a kind of stubborn pride that led to Andrew taking his son in. He clearly had little interest in the boy, but he'd be damned if someone else was going to raise him. The way Jeremy described his youth, it sounded almost like he was an employee rather than his father's son. Strict schedules, limited interaction and a handful of au pairs defined that time for Jeremy. On the surface, his needs were more than met. He never went hungry, always had the latest video games and the best sports gear. When he got his driver's license, Andrew gifted him a brand new Audi. It was a gesture that confirmed that even though his father didn't want to be emotionally invested, the outside world needed to know that he was good to his son.

Jeremy, being the paragon of openness that he was, had confided in Ava early about the troubles of his childhood and his strained relationship with his dad. Ava, attempting to counter as the optimist, thought that maybe things weren't as bad as he saw them. After all, people tend to see their own circumstances as more dire than they actually are.

Until she met him, that was.

When Jeremy finally relented and brought Ava over for dinner, Andrew was cordial enough, shaking her hand and politely making surface-level conversation during dinner. But she quickly got the sense that every compliment was backhanded, every sentence smattered with sarcasm. She was almost impressed at how he could so effortlessly pepper subtle vitriol into a conversation. It was so imperceptible that it was impossible to call him out on it. After they left, she couldn't pinpoint anything he said or did that was rude or out of line, it was just a vibe that emanated from a man she could tell was truly hateful deep down inside. Jeremy didn't disagree.

"That's just Andrew. He is what he is."

As time went on and the couple got more serious, they only saw him sporadically. When talk of marriage came up, he did nothing to try to dissuade them. He even said he'd pay for it because he knew Ava's parents weren't "people of means."

Ava often wondered if he took umbrage with her ethnicity or if he snubbed his nose at the fact that her family didn't have a lot of money while he probably wiped his ass with hundred-dollar bills (or at least she imagined he did), but ultimately, she realized that, for whatever reason, Andrew Carlisle was a deeply unhappy man who wanted everyone around him to be as unhappy as he was. So, ultimately, she realized the nicest thing she could say about Jeremy's dad was that he may be a dick, but at least he wasn't a bigot. He hated everybody equally.

Ava sighed in relief when the phone stopped ringing. She momentarily pondered clearing the missed call notification, but decided against it. She wasn't going to start off her marriage by dabbling in deception, no matter how minor or how noble her intentions. She resumed gathering their belongings as the sound of the shower ceased.

Jeremy exited the bathroom a few minutes later, wrapped in a towel in a repeat of yesterday morning. Like yesterday, he could immediately tell that something was off with his wife.

"You good?"

Ava didn't look at him as she noticed a pair of flip-flops jutting out from under the bed. She retrieved them and unzipped the suitcase enough to shove them in before re-sealing it.

"Of course! Why wouldn't I be?"

Jeremy shrugged. He'd done enough prying for one weekend and wanted to end on a positive note. Ava tried not to grimace as the dark tones of John Williams's seminal score emanated from his phone once again. Now it was Jeremy's turn to sigh.

"For fuck's sake," he muttered, retrieving the device.

He held it in his hands while the music played. Ava recognized that the tone was nearing its end and hoped he'd simply opt not to answer it.

"Hello, Dad."

Ava couldn't make out exactly what Andrew was saying from across the room, but the muffled voice was definitely elevated, almost shouting.

"Dad—"

More yelling.

"Dad, will you—"

Still more yelling. She saw Jeremy struggling for the right words to halt the onslaught, but ultimately, he gave up and just let Andrew rant. After what seemed like an hour—in actuality only a couple minutes—the ranting ended, allowing Jeremy to reply.

"I don't know what you want me to tell you, Dad. We did it. That's all there is to it."

...

"I texted you because I thought you should know."

...

"Because I didn't want you making our wedding all about you."

...

"You know what? I don't care about your friends. You worry more about what they think than your own son!"

That was not received well; the angry man on the other end of the line got significantly angrier.

"You're embarrassed? Guess what, Dad, I'm embarrassed of you. What do you think of that?"

The voice became apoplectic.

"Fine, Andrew! I don't care. I really don't."

...

"Whatever you say, old man."

Ava watched Jeremy try to maintain his composure. He sat on the bed, hanging his head low and clenching the phone in his hand while his jaw tightened. That conversation was the culmination of years of his dad being cold, detached and quietly abusive. She saw the wave of emotions twist his face as he continued his attempt to hold it together. But when the tears pooled at the bottom of his eyes, he lost it and spiked his phone into the hotel room carpet like he just scored the winning touchdown in the Super Bowl. The device shattered into an impressive number of pieces; modern cellular phones were clearly not as well-crafted as they used to be. A Nokia from the early 2000s would have probably put a hole in the floor.

Jeremy flopped back on the bed and rubbed his face with his palms. "Probably shouldn't have done that."

Ava came and sat down next to him, putting her arm around him. "Dare I even ask?"

"I texted him and told him we got married. He didn't appreciate finding out that way."

"Why didn't you wait until we got home?"

"What would it have mattered? He would have had the same reaction. Better we weren't in the same room when he did. Guess it was a bit of a cop-out on my part."

"I'm so sorry, baby."

Jeremy shrugged. "Fuck it. I knew this day would come eventually. The old bastard never did anything except throw money at me to keep me quiet. We're better off without him."

Ava didn't know how to respond. He was definitely right. There was no scenario she saw for their lives in which Andrew played a major part. Still, he was pretty much the only biological family Jeremy had left. She didn't want him to feel alone, a thought that he must have somehow sensed, because he continued with: "I have you. That's all I need."

"I love you, Jeremy."

"I love you, too."

They kissed.

"But we'll have to use your cell phone until I can get a new one."

Ava cringed and gave him a sheepish smile.

"Yeah, about that..."

Jeremy raised an eyebrow.

"I sort of forgot to pay my bill."

A little less than hour later, the newlyweds were sitting on a bench in front of the hotel, waiting for the valet to retrieve their car. Ava's leg was bouncing a mile a minute as she stared down the road, trying to somehow will their car to materialize.

"Ugh!" Ava said. "I never should have let you valet. We'd have been on the road by now if you'd self-parked!"

"Like we'd be better off lugging our suitcases all the way across the casino to the garage?"

"Uh, yeah."

Jeremy shook his head. Ava suspected that it wasn't about the luggage. She was sure he didn't want her overexerting herself. It irked her, but she wasn't about to have this old argument again, not after the episode with Jeremy's dad. Plus, she didn't need to be a mind reader to know he wasn't thrilled with her about the phone bill. He said he would have given her the money if she needed it, to which she assured him she didn't. She just forgot. Keeping up with due dates wasn't her strong suit; she'd much rather focus on less mundane tasks. Besides, she was never the type to be constantly glued to the screen. It wasn't unusual for her to just leave her phone at home when she went out. She wasn't great about keeping it charged either, both of which occasionally caused some friction with the man who was now her husband.

Still, she figured Jeremy couldn't exactly stay mad at her for not having a phone considering his was currently in several pieces in the hotel room wastebasket. They agreed that they'd stop at the first wireless store they passed on the way home to get a new phone for Jeremy and to pay Ava's outstanding bill to get hers turned back on.

She rested her head against his shoulder. Despite the tiny annoyances, she was happy. They were married and had a great weekend together, even though she didn't feel 100 percent by any means. In fact, she was feeling lightheaded again. She closed her eyes to stop the spinning, hoping it was just a hangover and not something worse. Her respite didn't last long as Jeremy's voice broke her concentration, sounding like it came from a dream.

"Car's here."

Ava popped on her sunglasses as they pulled out of the valet area and onto the street. Jeremy deftly worked his convertible through the traffic and onto the Atlantic City Expressway. They were quiet as they transitioned to the Garden State Parkway and then to Route 539. Ava always liked that road because it was long and quiet, lined with trees instead of the busy retail centers that bookended the roads as they got further north. About ten miles up there was a giant rock on the side of the road painted like the

American flag. She'd heard that it had been there as long as anyone could remember. In the 1990s, people had painted it differently every year—a pumpkin for Halloween or turkey at Thanksgiving time—but after September 11th, someone painted it with the stars and stripes and it remained that way ever since. It seemed that every time they drove by, there were more flags planted in the ground around it, along with signs like "Support Our Troops" and "God Bless the USA." It was a striking illustration of the difference between the chaotic hustle and bustle of North Jersey and the more rustic, rural southern part of the state.

She asked Jeremy to put the top down and he obliged, the warm breeze helping to ease her nausea.

She felt Jeremy's eyes on her and turned to him, offering a warm smile to assuage his concern. She didn't know if she'd love or hate the fact that he was always so in tune with how she was feeling. She appreciated it in this particular moment, but still tried to deflect.

"Feeling regret now that our honeymoon is over?" she asked.

Jeremy smirked. "I wouldn't exactly call that a honeymoon, but no. Not at all."

She smiled and reclined her seat. They rode in silence for a bit, having decided that the radio would be a bit much for their hangovers, especially since they tended to opt for heavier fare as opposed to the auto-tuned nonsense on mainstream radio: metalcore bands that assaulted their ears with guttural, screaming verses followed by soaring melodic clean vocal choruses. Bands like Atreyu, Ice Nine Kills, or Falling in Reverse. Ava especially gravitated toward female-fronted bands like Spiritbox, New Year's Day, or, her personal favorite, Butcher Babies. She loved that energy, but not right now.

Jeremy was the first to break the silence. "Fall semester is coming up. You think any more about going back?"

Ava didn't respond. She knew this was coming. She had been pursuing an associate's degree in special education at their local community college, but had stopped going a couple of years back, two semesters shy of graduating. She occasionally toyed with the idea of finishing up, but never too seriously. Jeremy, in his pestering, endearing way, often encouraged her to go back, at least to have the degree even if she didn't end up actually pursuing a career. She always claimed she was too busy, but that wouldn't have been a very convincing excuse even if it was the case. The truth was that she loved working with kids, but once she decided that she wouldn't have any of her own, the thought of working with other peoples' was somewhat less than appealing.

She changed the subject. "Did you ever hear from Inotech about their logo design?"

Although Jeremy's dream of drawing comic books never came to fruition, he did manage to utilize his artistic skills as a graphic designer, having taken on a number of small corporate clients over the past couple of years. Ava, of course, found his work spectacular and wasn't the least bit surprised at how well he had been doing recently, given his level of talent. This new job would be his most high-profile yet, but for some reason he didn't seem as enthused as she thought he'd be.

"Uh, not yet. I'll call them tomorrow."

"That should be a pretty well-paying gig, right?"

"Yup."

The terseness of his reply gave Ava pause.

"That's it?"

"What?"

"That's all you have to say about landing your biggest client yet?"

"It's just a job, babe. If I get it, I get it."

"Yeah, but—"

"But what?"

Ava lowered her sunglasses and glared at him. It wasn't like Jeremy to snap at her like that and she wanted him to know she had no intention of putting up with it.

"I'm sorry. Just still rattled by that shit with my... with Andrew."

"I get it, but don't take it out on me. It's not like you're relying on his money."

"No. I'm not. Not anymore."

The couple returned to silence. A low rumble began to materialize down the road behind them, Ava heard the sound, noting that it was louder than normal. Probably some douche in a souped-up muscle car trying to compensate for something. Unfortunately, they got that a lot in New Jersey, especially where they lived up north.

"You know my parents are going to want to celebrate, right?" Ava said, breaking the silence.

Jeremy smiled. "I'd expect nothing less. Think Mama would make her homemade ravioli?"

"If you ask her nice enough. You know she can't resist that bullshitter's smile of yours."

"You mean this one?" he said, exaggerating the look she described.

"Exactly."

"I guess I just have a way with the Allegretti wom..."

He trailed off as something caught his eye in the rearview mirror.

"What?" Ava asked.

Jeremy didn't take his eyes off the mirror. "Jesus Christ, this guy's in a hurry."

Ava turned and saw a black motorcycle quickly closing the distance between them, the roar of the engine growing exponentially louder as it closed on them. She couldn't quite make out any distinguishing features of its occupant, other than his clothes and helmet were as dark as his bike.

"Pull to the side a bit. Let him pass."

"Why should I?"

"You know how these biker guys are?"

"Like your ex-boyfriend?"

Ava giggled. "Oh, so we're doing the jealousy thing are we?"

"No."

"You're bigger if it makes you feel better," she said, reaching over and giving his crotch a playful squeeze.

Jeremy rolled his eyes, but acquiesced and glided slightly over to the right. The highway was only one lane each side, with the bisecting yellow line alternating between dotted and solid. A stretch of dotted lines was approaching, so Jeremy figured if he was in such a damn rush, he'd gladly let him go by.

Except he didn't.

The bike pulled up to the couple's bumper and stayed there, keeping pace with the car.

"What the fuck is he doing?" Jeremy said, exchanging a concerned look with his wife.

Ava turned again, getting a better look at the biker. His clothes were indeed all black, consisting of jeans and a long-sleeved T-shirt. His hands were concealed by a pair of worn leather gloves that tightly gripped the handlebars of his bike. He wore a leather vest, a look Ava was familiar with from the TV biker shows. He wore a half-helmet, the kind that covered his head but not much else. Despite that, his face was obscured by a pair of dark goggles and a face cover that blanketed his nose to his neck. It was like being followed by one of those evil cartoon soldier henchmen from G.I. Joe or something.

Ava threw up her hands at him. "Hey, asshole! Go around!"

She waved him past, but he stayed on their tail, not even giving the hint of moving.

"What the hell's your problem?"

Ava felt her courage draining. Even though she couldn't see the biker's face, she could somehow feel his eyes on her and it chilled her to the bone. She'd gotten her fair share of ogles from creepy men over the years, but something about this featureless husk on their tail creeped her out in a way she hadn't previously experienced.

She sat back in her seat and shot Jeremy a nervous glance. He tried to reassure her.

"It's okay. Just some asshole wannabe tough guy."

Jeremy turned and gave him the finger. Ava couldn't help but think that that it wasn't the smartest move. They felt a jolt as the motorcycle made contact with their bumper.

"What the *fuck?*" Jeremy shouted.

He slammed his foot down on the gas pedal and accelerated, temporarily putting some distance in between the couple and their pursuer. For a moment, the bike shrank into the distance, a false beacon of hope before it made up the lost ground in a matter of seconds. Instead of staying on their bumper this time, the biker pulled around to the driver's side, riding parallel with the convertible, keeping pace no matter how much Jeremy adjusted his speed.

Both vehicles were going dangerously fast now and Jeremy realized that he couldn't spare a glimpse in the biker's direction if he intended to stay on the road. Ava, however, didn't take her eyes off of him, noticing that his vest was old and worn. There were some rectangular spots toward the top that were less faded, as if there were patches that had been removed. She shuddered when she caught a glimpse of the machete sheathed on the side of the motorcycle. The Rider looked at her again, his obscured eyes presumably locked on to her. She still couldn't see them, but she felt them and the sensation she got nearly made her vomit. What the fuck did this guy want?

Ava turned to look at the road ahead, noting that the dotted lines had gone solid, indicating a curve up ahead.

"Jeremy, slow down."

Jeremy didn't answer. He was white-knuckling the wheel, trying his best to keep the vehicle under control.

"Jeremy!"

The curve approached as advertised and Ava screamed as a pickup truck came barreling into view. It was in the crazy biker's lane, placing him in the more immediate danger, but it was a threat to them too. Plus, even though this guy seemed like a nutcase, she didn't have any desire to see a motorcycle flattened by a truck while driving back from her honeymoon.

The truck's horn screamed at the Rider to get out of the way, but he stayed the course, plunging the driver into an unwitting game of chicken. What happened next took only a second, but it seemed unusually long, like when they talk about how football games slow down for quarterbacks after they've played for a while, allowing them to survey everything on the field in a matter of seconds.

She caught a glimpse of the truck driver's panicked expression. He clearly knew that he couldn't swerve into their lane, but it was also a risky proposition to veer off the road and onto the shoulder, putting him in peril of hitting a tree. The only other option was to run head on into the bike, also not a desirable outcome assuming the truck driver didn't want this nutjob's death on his conscience. His hands strangled the wheel, struggling to make a decision that he did not have time to make.

The Rider made it for him. He jerked to the left in an impossibly deft motion, narrowly missing the truck on the passenger side. Unfortunately for Jeremy, the Rider's maneuver caused the truck driver to instinctively jerk his vehicle toward his car, clipping the back driver's side bumper, sending them into a tailspin. Ava hoped Jeremy remembered his driver's education, which he clearly did, taking his foot of the gas and turning into the skid, gaining a precarious measure of control before attempting to brake, which only served to somewhat slow the car, but not stop it, unable to prevent it from barreling into a tall pine tree off the side. The airbags deployed upon impact, stunning Ava and Jeremy with the force of their inflation.

Ava didn't know how long it took her to regain her senses, but when she became lucid, she looked behind them to see the Rider stopped in the road, looking back over his shoulder at them. For the first time, she caught a glimpse of the patch on the back of his leather vest. It was a grinning skull dripping with blood. The logo above it said:

HELL'S HORDE M.C.

It looked like he was one of those so-called "outlaw bikers." She didn't know much about them besides what she saw on television. Movies and TV always depicted them as criminals who would get involved in drugs or gun running, but they weren't typically the type to go after the average person on the street, especially when they had no apparent connection. Why would this guy want to attack a random couple on the road? She felt like they had locked gazes for an eternity, even though she still couldn't see any of his features. She'd never seen this man before, but he had an eerie sense of familiarity about him. The outside world seemed to melt away as they engaged in their staring contest.

"Jesus Christ! Are you okay?"

Jeremy's voice broke her trance, but she didn't respond.

"Ava!"

She shook off the cobwebs and stole a glance at Jeremy to reassure him. "I'm okay"

"Are you sure?"

"Yes, I'm—"

She looked back toward the road and found herself entranced once again as the Rider dismounted his bike. He took a single step forward and stopped again, staring the wrecked vehicle down.

"What the fuck do you want?" Ava screamed in his direction.

The Rider tilted his head like a dog who understands his owner's inflection, but not the actual words. Ava heard the sound of tires screeching from the other direction and looked back to see the pickup truck speeding off. So much for exchanging insurance information. She heard the sound of metal clicking next to her and turned to see Jeremy struggling with his seatbelt, which was clearly stuck. Ava felt panic wash over her. What if this guy got that big-ass knife of his and came closer? What could they do to stop him? Especially if Jeremy was trapped? Was there anything on hand that she could use as a weapon?

The Rider stared at them for what felt like eons as Ava joined Jeremy as they frantically worked to free him from his seatbelt. When he finally moved again, it was not in the couple's direction. Instead, he turned around, mounted his bike and drove off into the distance, the howl of his engine fading as he sped away.

As he disappeared from sight, the seatbelt finally came loose, almost as if the Rider's very presence had held it closed. Jeremy embraced Ava tightly, hugging her as if he was afraid she'd fall over if he let go.

"Jesus Christ, baby! I didn't know what that guy was going to do!"

"I could feel him looking at me," Ava said. "It was like he was staring into my fucking soul or something."

Ava pushed away, knowing Jeremy wouldn't be the first to break the embrace. Not that she didn't want or need his comfort, but right now, she just wanted to get as far away from there as possible.

"Can you get out?" she asked.

"Yeah."

Jeremy looked over the hood; most of the damage was to the front of the car. Even though the airbags had deployed, they could still get out through the doors. They carefully maneuvered out of the vehicle, Jeremy surveying the damage.

"Motherfucker!" he shouted, observing the state of his vehicle. "I'll fucking kill that guy if he comes back."

He tried to sound convincing. He didn't.

Ava grabbed him by the hand and started leading him toward the trees.

"What are you doing?" Jeremy asked.

"We're getting away from here."

"All our stuff is in the car. We'll just call—"

The realization hit him hard. They'd just been in a car accident, there were no other vehicles around and neither one of them had a working phone.

"Do you have your wallet?" Ava asked.

"Yeah."

"Then that's all we need. We're going back this way, because that psycho went in that direction."

Jeremy took a look down the road before he stopped resisting Ava's push to move. She led him off the road and into the tree line, explaining: "I want to stay out of sight. If we hear a car coming we can flag them down. But if he comes back, I want to be far fucking away from here."

CHAPTER 3

Two days ago, Jeremy and Ava exchanged wedding vows. Today they found themselves traipsing through the woods after a car accident trying to avoid a lunatic biker. How quickly things can change.

While they were both undoubtedly shaken by the experience, neither one was significantly injured. Jeremy had a brush burn on his forehead from the airbag and Ava had bit her lip when it deployed, cutting it slightly. They were both moving on adrenaline, but Ava had a feeling that they would be very sore once they stopped and let their bodies process the trauma. She kept looking back, expecting to see the psycho pop out from behind a tree or a rock. She also listened intently, not only for the sound of that demon bike, but also for any cars that they could flag down for assistance.

In the twenty minutes they'd been walking, they'd heard only two vehicles approaching. One was going way too fast to signal and the other simply kept driving when the couple burst out of the woods, waving frantically to try to get its attention. It was hard to blame the driver for that. A couple of raggedy-ass kids popping out of the woods, trying to hitch a ride? No thanks. Ava was resigned to the fact that they'd just end up walking until they came to a convenience store, or God willing, a gas station.

She noticed that her chest was starting to feel tight and that breathing was becoming an issue. She tried her best to hide it, but to no avail.

"We should rest for a minute," Jeremy said.

"I'm fine."

"Ava..."

"I said I'm fine! I'm not stopping until we get somewhere safe."

"Ava!"

She stopped.

"I get it," Jeremy continued. "I want to get somewhere where there're people ASAP, but you need to rest."

"I don't need—"

"You have a fucking heart condition, Ava! And I'm tired of pretending you don't!"

"And I don't want to get murdered by a fucking maniac in the woods, so excuse me if my heart condition isn't my most pressing concern right now!"

She started to move forward again, but Jeremy grabbed her arm, probably harder than he intended.

She glared back at him, but something in his eyes told her not to protest on this one.

"Five minutes," he said matter of factly, displaying a calm authoritativeness that Ava was not used to.

Ava wrenched her arm away and walked over to the nearest tree, sliding down to the base. She took a deep breath, a labored action, harder than it should have been. She was pissed. Not pissed at Jeremy, but pissed that he was right. What good would getting away from that psycho do if her heart gave out? It was easy to put those thoughts out of her head exerting herself in the name of passion, but, out here, in what felt like very real danger, it was definitely closer to the top of her mind. She felt tears welling up in her eyes and did her damnedest to hold them back, but she couldn't. She put her hands over her face as the tears turned to sobs, a release of emotion she had fought to suppress for too long.

Jeremy came over and sat on the ground beside his wife and pulled her in close. Not saying anything, just letting her have the release she so sorely needed.

Ava ran track in high school. She was good. Very good in fact. Every day after school, whether in season or not, she would be on that track running. For Ava, it was not only exercise, it was like a drug to her. People always talked about the "runner's high" and, to Ava, it was a very real thing. She loved the freedom she felt when running in fresh air. No matter what problems she had at home or in school, no matter what mean things the other kids said about the "poor girl," when she ran, her problems were always behind her, becoming smaller in the distance, never able to catch her while the wind was at her back.

Until one spring afternoon when she was sixteen. It was a normal day. She felt great when she arrived at school that morning. When the bell rang, signaling the end of the day, she went to the locker room, changed into her athletic wear and started stretching on the track. As she did, she felt a twinge of pain in her upper abdomen. Nothing particularly alarming, but the discomfort was there. She wrote it off as byproduct of crappy cafeteria food. Dinners at the Allegretti household always consisted of fresh ingredients and generous helpings of vegetables. The same could not be said about the city's school lunch program. Ava did her best to choose the most nutritious options, but sometimes there wasn't enough variety. That particular day's frozen pizza was depressingly the most palatable selection. Ava was sure that was what she was paying for now as the pain ebbed.

She started her run and finished the first lap with no issue, which helped her forget about her earlier discomfort. It was a quarter of the way through her second go-round when she felt pressure building in her upper back. It was an odd sensation. She slowed, but didn't stop, wondering if she'd pulled a muscle or something. After a few more yards, breathing became difficult. Running had been a part of her life for a long time and it took a lot to get her winded, especially when she was only going at half speed like she was at the moment. Her stamina seemed almost completely gone and the fact that she was having trouble breathing scared her. She stopped and put her hands on her knees, trying to work through the respiratory episode, but she couldn't finish a breath no matter how hard she tried; her chest burned with each inhalation. She felt anxiety wash over her, bringing a wave of dizziness with it. She had never felt this sick in her life and her confusion and dismay stayed with her as she lost consciousness.

When she woke up in the hospital, Mama and Papa were there, trying but failing to put on brave faces. A series of tests followed over the next couple of weeks. Ava was never a hypochondriac, but all kinds of messed-up scenarios plagued her mind during that period. Was it cancer? Would she still be able to run track? Was she going to graduate? Fall in love? Get married? Have kids?

Eventually, the diagnosis came back.

Arrhythmogenic right ventricular dysplasia, or, as the doctor abbreviated it, ARVD.

The doctor explained everything in technical terms and was hard to follow at times, but the gist of it was that the right side of Ava's heart was weak and not pumping blood efficiently. This could lead to irregular heart rhythms. If she exerted herself too much, she would be at risk of sudden cardiac arrest. Not the news a sixteen-year-old track star would expect and it was as devastating to her parents as it was to her, especially because the doctor told them the condition was genetic and not the result of lifestyle choices. A hard pill for any parent to swallow, knowing that something in their DNA had resulted in their daughter's life being threatened.

What followed was a litany of doctors' visits and treatment options. The doctor put her on beta blockers, a medication designed to keep her heart rate in check. The problem was that they made her tired. Very tired. She would often come home after school and crash, sleeping through dinner on more than one occasion. Beyond the fatigue, her hands and feet were always cold. The doctor told her that was because the medicine slowed the blood flow to the extremities. All in all, it was a nightmare for her and, after a year, she just stopped taking them. Her parents were furious when they found out, but Ava stood strong. She had given up her athletic pursuits, but she wasn't going to be a slave to medication. Mama and Papa didn't like it, but they begrudgingly supported her once they realized that she was going to do this her way.

Her doctor was even less thrilled with the cessation. He said if she wasn't going to take the meds, then she should have something called an ICD implanted. He described it as an internal defibrillator, attached to her heart, so if it fell out of rhythm, the device would shock it back. Ava politely but firmly told him "No, thank you." She wasn't going to voluntarily get cut open. No way.

Ava decided that the best approach for her was to simply try to listen to her body. She wouldn't run track anymore, but she wouldn't shy away from going on a hike or other light exercise to stay in shape. She adjusted her diet to compensate for the lack of calories she'd burn. When she did physical activity, she'd stop it when she started to feel dizzy or short of breath. It required focus and dedication, but, for Ava, it was much better than relying on medication that often made her feel less than herself or, even worse, going in for surgery. She was convinced that if she went under the knife once, it would be a regular occurrence for the rest of her life.

When she met Jeremy, she did not disclose her condition right away. She'd done that with a previous guy who acted all understanding until he ghosted her before the third date. She wasn't sure if he didn't want anything to do with her health issues or if he was just a douche, but she didn't want to take the chance with this new guy. Something felt different about him from the very start. Once things started getting serious, they talked, as couples are wont to do, about their future. Jeremy expressed his desire to have kids. He said his dad was never involved, not even bothering to so much as show up at any of his sporting events. Jeremy vowed to be different. He wanted to coach every sport his kids played. Football, baseball, basketball. He didn't care. He even joked that he would coach cheerleading if need be. As Ava listened to his hopes and dreams, she felt sick to her stomach. She had decided and accepted that she would never be a mother not long after she went off the medication. So while listening to Jeremy opine about where he saw his life going, she knew it wouldn't be fair to drag him along if she wasn't in a position to help him achieve it. So, through tears bordering on sobs, Ava confessed that she was sick, which, in her mind, meant she was broken.

Jeremy listened with sympathy. He held her until the tears waned. After a long period of empathetic silence, Jeremy told her he loved her. He couldn't imagine a life without her and he would be fine wherever their journey took them as long as they were together.

It was a declaration that Ava never doubted, but Jeremy had often tried to sway her into at least considering the possibility of children.

"We have each other. It's not like it'd be on you to exert yourself with a baby."

His intentions were good, but he didn't get it. It wasn't necessarily the physical requirements of parenthood, it was the thought that she could die young, leaving not only the love of her life, but a child as well. The thought of putting people she loved through that trauma was unbearable to her.

Plus what if Jeremy remarried? She hated the thought of him spending his life with another woman. Throw a kid on top of that? The thought was intolerable. It wasn't that she didn't want him to be happy, but she loved him so much that she didn't want to ever be without him. She knew she would love her child in the same way and would mourn that hypothetical loss before it happened. That's why she initially thought about being a teacher, but eventually, even that was too heart-wrenching for her.

So now, sitting at the base of a tree in the woods off of State Highway 539 in southern New Jersey, leaning against her love, the emotion spilled out of her until she had no tears left to cry. When it was over, they sat in silence like they did on that night she first told him about her condition. Her sobs turned to sniffles and then to labored breaths, which continued for several minutes until they finally returned to normal. Another five minutes passed until she felt Jeremy's lips on her forehead, followed by his voice.

"Let's get going."

The couple continued their journey through the woods in silence. Ava felt better after her emotional release, but was all the more exhausted for it. They moved at a brisk-enough pace, which Jeremy managed, slowing them when he felt they were pushing too hard. Ava was still mad, but more so at her body's failings than Jeremy's concern. It wasn't her style, but she knew once they got home she'd have to take it easy for a couple of days at least.

Overall, their journey through the woods was only about forty minutes including the fifteen-minute cry break, but it felt much longer. It came to an end when they found a clearing in the trees, opening up to reveal their salvation—a full-service gas station.

"Holy shit," Jeremy said.

Ava took a deep breath. It stung a little, but the relief at not only finding a place with other people and a phone, but a gas station with a garage and a tow truck—"Eddie's Towing" was the less-than-creative name stenciled on the driver's side door—was a jackpot bigger than any they could have won at the casino. She picked up her pace as they emerged from the woods and moved toward the entrance. Jeremy didn't protest.

The gas station was small, consisting of only four pumps, two on each side, bisected by a small booth where the attendant sat. There wasn't even the convenience store typical of so many of these places throughout the state. It would have been nicer to stumble across a Wawa, but beggars couldn't be choosers.

Ava got nervous as they got closer. The mechanic's shop was dark inside and the door to the repair bay looked cracked and rusted. She looked for a sign to indicate whether it was at least in business, but found none.

"Is this place even open?" she asked, more to herself than to Jeremy.

Jeremy didn't answer right away as he surveyed their surroundings. "Yeah, there's someone in the booth."

Ava saw the silhouette of a man through the dirty glass. She broke into a light run to get closer. Jeremy reached out to grab her hand, but she eluded his grasp.

"Hey!" she yelled over to the man. "We need help!"

The man looked up from whatever it was he was doing and noticed the young lady running toward him. He stepped outside to see what the fuss was about.

Ava got a good look at him as he emerged from the enclosure. He was short and stocky. Not fat, but not exactly six-pack shredded either. He was a mass of bulky, undefined muscle like those guys from the strongman competitions. He looked like he could rip a phone book in half, but wasn't going to go shirtless on the cover of *Men's Health*. He wore a short-sleeve shirt exposing his arms, which were completely covered in tattoos from his biceps to his knuckles. One would surmise there were many more under his shirt. From a distance, you wouldn't even know he was bald, as his head was also covered in ink, forming a faux widow's peak.

A lot of people would be intimidated or put off by such a gruff-looking figure, but Ava wouldn't have been even if they didn't desperately need help.

"Are you Eddie?" she asked, slowing to a fast walk as she got closer.

The man eyed her up and down as he got a better look at her. Ava was too tired to even roll her eyes, but something about the way he looked at her gave her pause. It wasn't a leer. He actually looked confused. Even a little nervous. She decided that they must look rougher than they initially thought.

"How'd you know that?" Eddie asked.

"Lucky guess," Ava said, trying to curb her sarcasm as she pointed at the tow truck.

Eddie looked at his own vehicle dumbly, clearly not making the obvious connection right away. He turned back to her and stared. Not saying a word.

"Something wrong, man?" Jeremy chimed in.

The bewildered gas station attendant cocked his head, but still didn't respond.

"Dude!" Jeremy shouted.

Eddie looked at him. Ava thought maybe Jeremy had pissed him off, but he still just looked confused.

"Something wrong?" she asked.

Eddie finally broke his silence. "Nope. No problem here."

He sounded as if he was choosing his words deliberately. Like a disguised interrogation.

"Uh huh," Ava said.

"We were in an accident," Jeremy said.

Eddie didn't take his eyes off of Ava. "I can see that," he said. "Are you kids hurt?"

"We've been better," Ava replied.

Finally, Eddie seemed to be able to shake off whatever it was about Ava that had him all twisted up. "Shit, son. Where's your car?"

"A few miles up the road," Jeremy answered.

"Why the hell didn't you just call for a tow?"

Ava and Jeremy exchanged glances.

"Phone trouble," she said.

Eddie eyed them suspiciously. Ava couldn't blame him. Two twentysomethings without a cell phone between them wasn't the most believable of scenarios.

"Look, man," Jeremy said. "Can you help us or not?"

Ava sat in the middle of the tow truck's front seat, huddling as close to Jeremy as possible. This Eddie guy was acting really weird. Typically, she'd think it was something pervy, but she'd dealt with lechers before. This was something different. Something about her seriously freaked this guy out which, in turn, unsettled the hell out of her.

Eddie, clearly not being a great conversationalist, drove in silence, only speaking to confirm the car's location. Even though they had stayed off the road, Jeremy did a good job of keeping their bearings. It wasn't hard as the road was mostly a straight shot for several miles. After less than ten minutes on the road, Eddie spoke up.

"I'm guessing that's it."

Ava peered out through the windshield to see the wreck of Jeremy's car off-road where they had left it. She was surprised, having half-expected the scene to be crawling with police at this point, but in Jersey, it seemed like people never minded their own business except at times when they shouldn't. She wanted to make a smart-ass comment, but thought better of pissing off this inked-up weirdo who, for better or worse, was their best friend at the moment.

Eddie pulled the truck to the shoulder and the trio exited, heading down to observe the damage.

"Shit, you really did a number on your ride, kid."

"Wasn't our fault," Jeremy said.

"I can see that," Eddie replied, pointing at the front of the wreckage.

"What are you..." Ava started to say, but stopped as she covered her mouth to stifle a scream.

A dead buck was splayed out the hood of the car, its stomach sliced completely open. Its insides sloughed through the broken windshield and into the front seat, pooling up with blood from its throat which, like its abdomen, had also been cut wide open.

"You guys really did a number on Bambi here."

"We didn't hit a deer!" Jeremy said.

"Someone should tell him that," Eddie said gesturing to the massacred buck.

"Some crazy fucker on a motorcycle ran us off the road," Ava said. "He must have come back and left this thing on our car. Fucking psycho!"

She looked at Eddie and noticed that the color had drained from his face. "A motorcycle?" he asked, his voice cracking.

"Yeah, a fucking motorcycle," Jeremy said. "He was wearing one of those vests with the patches. Guess he's part of a club. Hell's Horde or some shit. You ever hear of them?"

"No." Eddie said. A little too quickly in Ava's estimation.

"You run a gas station, but you've never come across the local biker club?"

"I said no," Eddie snapped

Jeremy and Ava exchanged a glance, unconvinced.

"Listen, man," Jeremy said. "If you know something about these guys..."

"No, *you* listen, kid," Eddie said. "I told you I don't know shit about any M.C. around here."

"You certainly know the lingo," Ava said, too pissed to hide her sarcasm.

Eddie sighed heavily. He looked very anxious and was starting to sweat.

"I can't do shit about this car with no dead deer practically in the front seat. Gonna have to call... animal control... or some shit."

"Are you fucking serious?" Jeremy said.

"Yeah. I'm fucking serious."

Eddie turned and headed back to his truck.

"You just going to leave us here?" Ava asked.

"If you want a ride, there's a diner a couple miles that way. You can call for help there."

The couple didn't even know how to respond. There was clearly something this guy wasn't telling them. They watched as he got in and started the truck.

"It's going to be dark soon, kids. My offer to drive you to the diner expires in thirty seconds."

Ava glanced back at the car. She didn't want to get back in the truck with Eddie, but the thought of ending up like that poor animal was significantly less appealing. They reluctantly got back in the truck, barely getting the door shut before Eddie peeled off down the road.

CHAPTER 4

Eddie pulled the tow truck back up to the garage and quickly got out, eyeing his surroundings. The sun was halfway down and it would be dark soon. He knew he didn't have a lot of time. What was the deal with that girl? She looked so much like...

He didn't finish his thought as the familiar rumble of a motorcycle emerged from down the road. His heart sank and his balls shriveled at the sound.

He burst through the door of the garage, making a point not to turn on any of the lights. There was still enough sun to see what he was doing as he made his way to the office, specifically to the safe under the desk. Eddie's fingers fumbled with the combination, screwing up twice trying to get it open, all while the sound of the bike grew louder.

"C'mon, motherfucker!" he muttered through gritted teeth.

Finally, he got it open on the third try. He pulled the nine-millimeter pistol out and checked the clip. It was loaded. He chambered a round, not even bothering to shut the safe which at this point only contained his cut: Hell's Horde M.C. A garment he hadn't donned in years. Not since that night. That fucking girl. How was this possible?

Eddie was rattled, a feeling he hadn't felt in a long time. Not since...

Eddie heard the bike pull up to the garage and stop, the engine still idling, a sound somehow both familiar and foreign at the same time. Eddie couldn't remember the last time he'd been on a bike. Once the Horde fell apart, the idea lost its luster. Plus, the first few months after everything went down, he was afraid the cops would show up at his door asking questions. He was known to local law enforcement, but that didn't mean he couldn't keep a low profile. He ditched the cut and sold the bike. He started working at the gas station.

After a few months, old man McLeary found out just how good he was at tuning up engines. Moved him from attendant to mechanic where he worked for years until McLeary stroked out on the shitter one fine autumn evening.

Eddie was shocked to find out that the geezer had left the shop to him. He knew McLeary wasn't married and he had mentioned something about a kid he'd had with some hippie chick somewhere out west, but, for some reason, he saw Eddie like a son. Not that the old man was liberal with affection or even a kind word, but there was definitely a quiet respect and admiration. Eddie's eyes actually started welling up at the thought. Through his misspent youth to his waste of an adulthood, that old dude was the only one who ever saw anything other than failure in him.

The cycle continued to idle outside, the sound reminding Eddie that this was definitely not the time for reminiscing.

He let the pistol lead the way as he slowly crept toward the front of the garage. That son of a bitch was out there. He knew this day would come, no matter how impossible it seemed. Everyone wanted to tell themselves that it was over all those years ago, but Eddie knew better. He knew the bill would come due eventually and the collector was right outside his door.

As he approached the window, he confirmed his suspicion. The bike was unmistakable. A custom job that was, in Eddie's humble opinion, his best work ever, even though it had been more than two decades since he'd done it. It somehow looked just as good as the day he finished building it. But the Rider was nowhere to be seen.

Eddie's thoughts crept up on him again. He figured this is what it was like when people describe their lives flashing before their eyes in situations of imminent danger. He looked at that motorcycle, a mechanical steed carrying what he knew was his own personal angel of death and lamented that his only notable accomplishment was building that bike. No wife, no kids, no legacy other than a rickety old service station that he hadn't even opened himself. He'd had nothing in his life outside of his time with the club and now, if he were to die tonight, he would die as he lived. With nothing.

Eddie thought about heading out directly into the confrontation, but it felt like a setup. There weren't a lot of places for someone to hide, but he couldn't see everything. Hell, the bastard might even be just on the other side of the door.

"It's you. Isn't it?" he yelled through the door.

No reply.

"I got a nine pointed right at that fucking door, so don't even think about trying to come in here."

The deafening silence persisted. Eddie thought about shutting up himself, but he figured trying to talk his way out of this gave him a better chance of still breathing when the sun came up tomorrow.

"This is about that girl, right? I know she looks just like her, man. I saw her too. Couldn't fucking believe it."

Still nothing.

"I can tell you where she is. I do that, we square?"

Eddie felt a lump in his throat as the Rider stepped into view of the window. He was covered head to toe, still wearing his helmet, goggles and face cover. He couldn't make out a single feature, but there was no doubt that he was exactly who Eddie thought he was. He saw the machete in his hands, streaked with blood, probably from the deer. He hoped it was just from the deer. Eddie trained his gun on the silent figure, aiming square at his chest. If he had to fire, he wanted to drop him with the first shot.

"It was you that did Micah, right? Chopped his goddamn head off in the Barrens?"

The Rider didn't respond. Eddie concluded that he wouldn't, no matter what he said.

"Lola's diner. I dropped the girl and her man there fifteen minutes ago. They're probably still there. You can definitely catch them if you leave now."

The Rider turned his head, looking down the road in the direction of the diner. Eddie thought about taking the shot, but opted not to. He heard about the way they found Micah's headless body in the woods a few weeks back. The papers didn't say much, but word gets around in some of the seedier circles. When you choose a certain life, there's bloodshed involved, but the brutality of the crime indicated someone had it out for this guy in a bad way. And Eddie knew, no matter how impossible it seemed, that there was only one person who hated Micah that much.

As the Rider turned back, Eddie raised his hands, taking the gun off of him.

"She's there. I ain't bullshitting you, man."

The Rider continued to stare. Eddie felt his anxiety rise as the standoff dragged out. The door was locked, but his counterpart could easily bust through the window. It was becoming clear to him that he was going to have to become the aggressor to get out of this. He trained the gun back on the man on the other side of the window.

"It don't have to go down like this, brother."

Maybe it didn't. The Rider turned and walked back to his bike, mounting it. Eddie's heart was in his throat as he watched him back up his ride. He started to pull onto the highway, but stopped and turned abruptly toward the pumps. He dismounted and grabbed one of the nozzles.

"What the fuck is he doing?" Eddie thought. "Gassing up?"

If only it were that simple. The Rider extended the hose as far it could go, spraying gasoline all over the ground.

Eddie panicked, almost pulling the trigger, but thankfully remembered that bullets and gasoline don't mix. The Rider turned the nozzle toward the tow truck, dousing it. The control to the pump was in the booth. He couldn't get to it without confronting the Rider, a dicey proposition considering he couldn't fire his gun. His only option was to run out the back and into the woods. Fuck. That hadn't gone well for Micah, but he didn't have much of a choice. He ran to the back as the Rider soaked the windows, the smell penetrating the cracked walls of the garage and making Eddie dizzy. He slammed into the rear door, pain shooting through his shoulder as it didn't budge. He pushed against it again, trying futilely to open it. If he could see the other side, he would be aware of the large tree branch recently wedged under the doorknob preventing his escape.

"No!"

Eddie was a hard man. He'd been in more fights than he could remember, even sending a couple unfortunate fellas down for a dirt nap. But now, trapped in this garage, facing a gruesome fate, tears began to stream down his face, a sensation he hadn't felt since before he got his ball hairs. He slumped to the door, waiting for it to end. But it didn't. The splashing of the gasoline stopped and the motorcycle revved back up. He heard it ride off down the road.

He was stunned that he was still alive. Maybe the Rider was just sending him a message.

Eddie struggled to his feet and carefully made his way to the window. He looked out to see the pump on the ground, still leaking gas. The bike and its occupant were nowhere in sight, but he did see the other four pumps were all sliced open, spurting petrol all over the site. He hesitated, but turned the knob in an attempt to exit.

The front door was blocked as well.

Eddie tried several times to push it open to no avail.

What the hell?

Suddenly, the sound of the bike returned and grew very loud, very quickly. Eddie rushed over to the workbench and grabbed the heaviest wrench available. He threw it at the window, shattering the glass. The putrid smell of the gasoline infected the garage without the barrier. Eddie climbed out in time to see the Rider coming back down the road, his machete drawn.

Eddie stumbled as he exited, but managed to keep his balance. He froze as the Rider turned back into the gas station. He expected him to come right for him, but instead, he looped around the pumps, dragging the machete across the ground as he did. Eddie's eyes expanded as he saw the sparks fly from the blade as it met the concrete.

The last thing he ever saw was the giant wall of flame that engulfed him as the pumps exploded.

Chapter 5

Ava and Jeremy sat in the booth at Lola's, waiting for their meals. It was a nondescript railcar-style diner with a barrel vault roofline and black-and-white checkered tiles on the floor. The chrome-plated red swivel stools lining the counter sat mostly empty save for an old man sitting midway down, sipping on coffee while neglecting a half-eaten meatloaf dish in front of him. He was too caught up in his newspaper to be bothered with anything else. It made Ava think of her father. Papa was the only person she knew who still read a newspaper every morning. Across from the counter, which was the restaurant's most prominent feature, booths lined the wall, again mostly empty, except for another couple in the furthest booth from the door. They were older than Ava and Jeremy and were trying to carry on a conversation, which must have been tough since they were constantly looking around, reading as more than a little paranoid. The fact that the woman was wearing a wedding ring while the man was not might offer a reason for their secrecy.

Ava and Jeremy were exhausted and more than a little freaked out. The waitress behind the counter had eyed them suspiciously when they first walked in. After all, they were bruised, bloody and dirty from the combination of the accident and the trek through the woods. She was an older lady, smelling of cigarettes and vodka, probably sneaking an occasional swig from the flask that bulged out of her apron, fooling no one. Her yellowed and faded name tag identified her as "Bethany."

"Holy hell, what happened to you two?" She had asked after they had shuffled in from the muggy night air.

Jeremy explained that they had been in an accident and didn't have a phone. He left the finer details—like the crazy biker, the mutilated deer and the oddball tow truck driver—out of the explanation. Ava could tell that Bethany wasn't totally buying it. Probably thought they were on drugs or something. She wouldn't let them actually use the phone, but she would call the police for them. Ava admired her thought process. After all, if they were some kind of modern-day Mickey and Mallory, she could guarantee the cops would actually show up. Jeremy thanked her and said they'd wait outside. She softened up a tad when he said it.

"No need for that. You must be hungry. Why don't you grab a booth and Courtney over there will take care of you."

Courtney was young. Younger than Ava by her estimation, but was pretty in a natural way. Unlike Bethany, her name tag was a brighter white, having clearly not been employed at this fine establishment as long as the older woman. She was slim except for her bulging belly. It wasn't polite to assume and you definitely shouldn't ask, but the girl was clearly a few months pregnant. She smiled and waved the couple over to a booth.

"Hi and welcome," she said in a gratingly pleasant tone that hit Ava like nails on a chalkboard. She normally would have felt bad for being so irritated at someone for just being nice, but she was too tired and achy to care.

"Oh, and don't get confused," Bethany called over. "You are expected to pay. This isn't a charity."

Jeremy pulled his credit card from his pocket and flashed it at Bethany. She nodded and went back to attending to the other patrons.

They ordered a couple of cheeseburgers and disco fries, an area staple which consisted of French fries smothered in gravy and cheese. Courtney dutifully wrote down their order and sashayed back to the kitchen, placing the ticket on the order wheel, giving it a playful spin before shouting to the back. "Order up, Chuck!"

The window at their booth overlooked the parking lot and the couple kept their eyes glued to the road outside, hoping the next vehicle to arrive would be a police car and not a motorcycle. They could see enough road in both directions, but it was getting darker, reducing the visibility by the moment. Only a single streetlight illuminated the front of the parking lot. An image popped into Ava's head of the psycho standing in the light like he was in some kind of sadistic stage play, his blade unsheathed and resting at his side. She shivered at the thought.

Jeremy reached over and took Ava's hand, startling her from her trance. She blinked and looked again at the front of the lot, seeing only the gravel in the light. She gave his hand a squeeze of her own.

"You okay?" Jeremy asked.

"I will be as soon as the cops get here."

"I know."

"Why was that Eddie guy so freaked out? I mean, he clearly knew something about that biker. You think they were in the same club?"

Jeremy shrugged. "Could be. He definitely looked the part. Maybe the cops know something about it."

Ava nodded and looked down at her hands, realizing just how dirty they were.

"I'm going to use the restroom. Try to clean up a bit."

"Good idea. I'll wait here until you get back in case the police show up in the meantime."

She got up and gave his hand a squeeze before letting go. She asked Courtney where the bathroom was. The waitress beamed another annoyingly cheerful smile as she pointed to the back. Ava headed off.

Ava looked at herself in the mirror. No wonder Bethany had given her such a look when they first walked in. Her hair was disheveled and frizzed from the mixture of humidity and sweat, and she had a pretty sizable bruise on her forehead. Dried blood smeared her chin from the cut on her lip. She ran her hands under the water. She splashed some on her face. The cold water was a shock, but it felt good. Woke her up a bit. She grabbed some paper towels and cleaned off the blood, taking care to dab gently when she got to the cut on her lip. It stung like hell as she cleaned it.

When she was satisfied that her face was as good as it was going to get, she washed her hands with a generous amount of soap. She wanted to get rid of the dirt, but also to be careful they didn't get too dry. They already hurt, and she was trying to avoid drying them out to the point of cracking the skin.

She looked back up at the mirror and gasped.

The reflection staring back at her wasn't her own, not really. The woman in the mirror looked almost exactly like her, but her hair was straight and shaved on the sides, a style Ava had never rocked herself. There were no bruises and no dirt. She was wearing dark eyeshadow and a blood-red shade of lipstick. Two dagger-shaped earrings hung from her lobes, not the small studs Ava usually wore. The tank top she'd put on that morning was gone, replaced by a low-cut Harley Davidson T-shirt. She was also wearing a black choker-style necklace.

Ava shut her eyes tight, confused at the macabre yet strangely familiar sight in front of her. She willed them to stay shut until her mind was able to decipher that perhaps it was just the trauma of the day's events coupled with pain and exhaustion that were resulting in the hallucination. When she opened her eyes again, she was sure it would be her own reflection looking back at her.

It wasn't.

Her doppelganger was still there, except now the choker necklace was gone. At first, there was nothing out of the ordinary about the girl's neck, but soon a thin line appeared, seemingly out of nowhere. Ava's confusion turned to terror as the girl behind the glass tilted her head back, widening what her viewer now realized was a gaping throat wound. Blood started to flow out, a languid trickle at first. But it didn't take long for it to gush forth, coating her skin in a crimson sheen. Her mirror-twin's mouth was wide in an attempt to scream, but no sound was audible. Her eyes pleaded with Ava, a mixture of fear and agony. She reached out, grasping for help, but the neck wound started spurting out, splashing the mirror from the ethereal plane inside. Ava recoiled, expecting the girl's blood to hit her, but it didn't. It sluiced down the mirror until it was completely red, masking her double from view.

Ava stifled a scream and stumbled backward against the door, wincing in pain as the handle jabbed into her lower back, causing her eyes to close involuntarily.

This time when she opened them, the woman in the mirror was gone and it was her own familiar, bruised and weary face looking back at her.

What the hell was going on here?

Ava took a moment to compose herself. The last thing she wanted to do was come out of the bathroom looking rattled, but she also wanted to get the hell out of there as soon as she could. Had she hit her head? Was this some kind of concussion symptom? Or something related to her heart? She stopped to wonder if her blood was pumping properly. She could feel her heart rate elevated from the shock, but she didn't feel that it was dangerously out of rhythm as far as she could tell.

She took a deep breath and exited the bathroom. As she made her way back to the booth, she noticed a new patron at the counter. He was tall and burly, probably in his mid to late fifties. He had long, stringy brown hair and a mostly gray beard with a length somewhere between Santa Claus and Gandalf. His clothes were nondescript, if a little on the dirty side. A simple pair of jeans and a black T-shirt. His arms were tatted up, but not to the extent of Eddie the tow truck driver.

She must have caught his eye as she passed because he did a double take. Ava was in no mood, so she shot him a glare.

"Can I help you?"

"I know you from somewhere?" the man asked sounding more like a statement than a question.

"Doubt it," Ava replied as she made her way back to the booth.

She slid in across from Jeremy and saw that the fries were on the table. She snatched three off the top, a stringy rope of cheese connecting it to the plate until it broke just before she popped it into her mouth. She finished chewing and smiled at her husband, hoping he wouldn't pick up on how freaked out she had been in the bathroom.

"Shit, that's good," she said. "Can't believe how hungry I am."

"What's up with Mr. Friendly over there?" Jeremy asked nodding toward the man at the counter.

"Who the hell knows? I'm so tired of people acting weird tonight." She chomped on two more fries and glanced out the window, furrowing her brow. "And where are the cops?"

Jeremy didn't answer. He was looking behind her. She heard the voice before she turned around.

"You kids in some sort of trouble?"

Ava looked back to see the man from the counter standing behind her. Something about the way he looked at her sent a shiver up her spine. It was clear that he really thought he knew her somehow. Why was this becoming a fucking trend tonight?

"No trouble, buddy," Jeremy replied. "All good here."

"Then why y'all waiting for the cops?"

"Car trouble," Ava said, hoping her brevity would not be lost on him.

"Car trouble," the man parroted. "Wouldn't you be better off calling a tow truck than the police?"

"Seems like you don't want the police showing up here," Ava said. "You got a warrant or something?"

"Not that I'm aware of," the man said, leaning over the table and bracing himself on the corners. "I just can't seem to place how I know you."

Ava didn't believe him. He knew more than he was letting on.

"You from around here?"

"Listen, man," Jeremy said, "We had a long night and are just waiting for the cops so we can get home."

Ava chimed in. "So, if you don't mind..."

She stopped when she caught a glimpse of the man's forearms. Specifically, a tattoo. More specifically, a tattoo of the same skull that was emblazoned on the crazy biker's vest.

"What the hell?"

Bethany looked over from behind the counter and narrowed her eyes at the scene. "There a problem over there, Bobby?"

"Not at all, sweetheart," Bobby replied, eyeing the young couple. "Right, kids?"

Something told Ava they shouldn't make a scene. The cops would be there any minute. No sense riling this guy up. If he was in the same crew with that other biker, he could be dangerous. Plus, it seemed like he was a regular here. He probably wouldn't try anything in public with witnesses.

She hoped.

"No problem, ma'am," Jeremy called over to Bethany.

"Appreciate the concern, sweetheart," Bobby said.

"I told you to cut out that sweetheart shit," Bethany replied. "I need a cigarette." She pulled a partially crumpled pack of some brand Ava wasn't familiar with and went outside with a huff, adding, "All kinds of crazy folks out tonight."

Bobby took the couple's cooperation as an invitation to sit. He slid into the booth next to Ava, who instinctively moved as far down as she could. He grabbed a handful of fries, grease and cheese dripping into his beard as he piled them into his mouth.

"What do you want, man?" Jeremy asked, trying his best to sound intimidating.

"I want to know why you two are sitting in a diner waiting for the cops, looking all banged up like you are."

"Why don't you ask your friend?" Ava said with a sneer.

"Don't got friends."

"So your tattoo matching the vest of the asshole that ran us off the road is a fucking coincidence?"

Bobby swallowed like he had the largest lump in the world stuck in his throat. It was as if he expected the answer, but was still afraid of it. Like a cancer patient getting a terminal diagnosis.

"Do you have a ride?"

"Didn't you hear?" Jeremy said, "We were in an accident. We're waiting for the cops."

"Listen," Bobby said, "you need to get as far away from here as possible right now."

The couple exchanged a nervous glance.

"I know this is going to sound crazy, but I got a truck out back. You come with me and I'll drive you away from here."

"What are you talking about?" Ava asked. "Who is that guy? Some kind of rival?"

"Nothing like that. Nothing to do with me at all, truth be told."

"Then what is this about? Why did he run us off the road?"

"You got something he wants. I didn't think this day would ever come, but I knew it as soon as I saw you."

"What does he want?"

"I'll explain in the truck, but we have to get out of here right fucking now."

He got up and grabbed Ava by the forearm, not too hard, but firmly.

Jeremy stepped in and yanked his grip away from her. "Just hold the fuck up..."

"No, you hold the fuck up, son. You have no fucking idea the shit you're in."

Jeremy held the man's wrist and glared at him. "No, I don't, but if you think we're going anywhere with you, you're just as crazy as the other guy."

"You have no idea about the 'other guy.'"

At this point, Ava became aware that the other patrons were glued to the scene.

Courtney hesitantly made her way over to try to diffuse. “Bobby, what is going on?”

“This don’t concern you, darling.”

“You’re making a scene. Bethany ain’t gonna be happy about this.”

“I’m trying to help these folks.”

Jeremy scoffed as he released the larger man’s wrist. “You got a funny way of—”

He didn’t get to finish his thought as the next sequence of events happened so fast, it was impossible to tell which came first. If they could somehow slow time, the first indicator would have been Courtney’s eyes bulging as she looked past them and out the window next to the booth. Next came a deafening boom emanating from directly outside their window, followed by the shattering of the glass. Shards rained down on the three of them in the booth as they instinctively ducked for cover.

While they attempted to shield themselves, Courtney’s head exploded. A sickening assemblage of blood, scorched flesh, broken teeth and brain matter burst from her neck to paint the wall behind the counter. Ava screamed when she saw that the only thing left of the young girl’s pretty face was the lower half of her jaw. Her tongue, surprisingly still intact, dangled obscenely from the stump. A geyser of blood spurted from the ruined woman’s neck like a fucked-up fountain as her body swayed on its feet for several seconds before crumpling to the ground, leaking over the tile floor.

As the trio in closest proximity to the gruesome scene tried to process their shock, the other patrons jumped from their seats and instinctively ran for the door. A previously unseen line cook bolted from the kitchen—he must have been Chuck. As that area was closest to the exit, he was the first one to it. Before he could fling open the doors to freedom, a dark shape burst through, knocking them off their frames, sending more aluminum and glass spraying. The husk smacked into the skinny cook like a wrecking ball, sending him barreling back toward the kitchen.

It took a second, but Ava recognized the shape as Bethany, or what was left of her.

As the cook pushed the dead woman off him, Ava saw that her head was completely twisted around. It was like the scene in *Spaceballs* where Mel Brooks's head is on backward after getting beamed to the other room. Except there was nothing comical here. The woman's blank eyes were wide open, having seen something unthinkable just before she died. A jagged piece of bone protruded from her throat. It didn't take a medical examiner to know that her head hadn't gotten that way gradually.

The cook screamed as the Rider emerged from the night into the diner, brandishing his machete in one hand and a sawed-off shotgun in the other. One of those double-barreled deals. More than likely the instrument that had obliterated Courtney's head. The scream became a gurgle as the Rider brought the machete down on the man's head, splitting it from his cranium to the bridge of his nose.

A scream came from behind Ava. It was from the woman with the man in the other booth. The Rider didn't even look away from his most recent kill as he raised the shotgun and blew a hole right through her chest, showering her companion with crimson. Now it was his turn to scream. The Rider dislodged the machete from the cook's ruined face and, in one deft motion, flung it at the man. It spiraled end over end in the air, hitting him in the top of his chest, knocking him back into the booth. He reached up, attempting to dislodge the blade, an attempt that proved both feeble and futile. His hands collapsed to his sides as he died.

Ava knew they had to get out of there but was paralyzed by the shock of what was going on around her. Fortunately, Bobby was with it enough to act. He grabbed a stool from the counter and heaved it at the broken window, widening the gap and clearing some of the larger, jutting shards so they could fit through.

"Go!" he ordered the couple as he pushed Ava toward the window.

Instinct took over and she vaulted through the opening, a feat of athleticism she hadn't performed since her track days. Jeremy followed suit, not as gracefully, but he successfully made it out. Bobby was next, stumbling and hitting the ground hard. Jeremy helped him to his feet.

"My truck's there," Bobby said, pointing to an old brown jalopy in the corner of the lot.

They ran to the vehicle, but Ava looked back to see where their pursuer was. She saw the old man from the counter, trying to mimic their escape through the window, only for the Rider to catch him by his shirt. The monster pulled him back against his chest and reached around to grab his throat with a gloved hand. He ripped the wrinkled flesh from the terrified man's throat like it was tissue paper.

"Come on, Ava!" Jeremy shouted.

She turned back and Jeremy ushered her into the truck. She slid into the middle seat, no longer concerned about her proximity to Bobby as she had been with Eddie, as Jeremy got in beside her. Bobby jumped into the driver's seat and revved the old vehicle up. Ava was both surprised and relieved that it started as quickly as it did. As they pulled out of the parking lot, she took another look back at the diner.

The Rider stood in the window, the dead man slumped over, half in and half out, his blood painting the outside. He watched as they sped away.

CHAPTER 6

"Fuck! Fuck! Fuck!"

Ava shouted the staccato expletives as she became acutely aware that she was covered in blood. The sensation came to her first as she realized that her tank top clung wetly to her skin. She brought her hands up to her sight line and confirmed that they were indeed red and sticky. She pulled the gore- and sweat-soaked garment away from her skin and held back a retch as a tooth fell down from the top and became trapped against her belly. She instinctively pulled the bottom of the shirt away and let the foreign object fall to the ground and under the passenger seat of the pickup. She knew the tooth wasn't hers—likely the ill-fated young waitress whose head had burst like a watermelon in front of her only a few minutes earlier—but she still ran her tongue over her own behind her lips. Just to be sure.

Bobby's pickup was old and rickety. It was absolutely pushing the limits of its horsepower and Ava felt sick to her stomach knowing that it was not moving fast enough. She had seen that motorcycle move. It was an old-fashioned chopper, but it zoomed down the road like a sport bike. It might have even been faster than that. There was no sign of him yet, but it wouldn't be long before he appeared behind them. She was sure of it.

The cab was disgusting. Ava wasn't a snob, but the level of filth inside this vehicle was epic. The seats were tattered and stained with God knows what, but considering she'd just taken a bath in young Courtney's brains, and the fact that this was their only option for escape, put this ride squarely in the "beggars can't be choosers" category. The smell of blood invaded her nostrils, making her feel ill again. She looked at Jeremy and then turned to Bobby. All three of them were covered. The thick gobs hanging from Bobby's beard were especially nauseating. Ava imagined that the cab would not have smelled great even if they weren't soaked in viscera. In fact, she wondered if this truck was actually Bobby's home. The smell of the blood mixed with the foulest stale locker room stench she could imagine—like a sweat sock stuffed with shit.

But none of that mattered. She didn't even know if they should trust this man. After all, he was clearly connected to this psycho biker in some way. Still, he wasn't actively trying to kill them at the moment so that would have to be enough. At least until they made it to safety.

Safety. She couldn't remember the feeling of security, even though this ordeal was only a few hours old.

Jeremy swiveled his head back and forth, looking out the back window for signs of pursuit and scanning Ava up and down for injuries.

"Are you okay?" he asked.

"No, I'm very fucking far from okay."

"I know, but are you hurt? Is any of that... yours?"

Ava was fairly confident it wasn't but looked herself over just in case. "No... Jesus Christ. That girl..."

She was shocked that the shotgun had taken the girl's head off like that. She was familiar enough with guns from movies and video games to know that a shotgun tended to be less accurate from a distance, but the killer wielded that thing with inhuman precision.

"Wrong place at the wrong time," Bobby's raspy voice came from her other side.

"Who the fuck is that guy?" Jeremy interrogated. "You clearly know him."

"I knew a guy. That ain't no guy. That's something else entirely."

"What does that mean?"

"It means that I knew a guy that looked like that. That rode that bike. That wore that cut. No doubt that's him, but there's no way it can be."

"You're not making any sense, man."

"What is he?" Ava interjected, furiously punctuating each word.

"A dead man."

"He just took out a whole diner full of people with no effort at all and you're going to take him out?"

"That ain't what I mean."

Jeremy and Ava exchanged a glance and turned back to Bobby who answered without them posing the question.

"He's been dead for twenty years."

The couple had every intention of asking follow-ups to determine exactly what the fuck this crazy man was talking about, but they didn't get the chance as the unmistakable sound of a motorcycle rapidly escalated in volume behind them.

Ava's stomach spun in sickening circles as the sound of the pursuing bike got closer to the barely functional jalopy that was their only hope for escape. She couldn't bring herself to turn around, but she did steal a glance across Jeremy at the side mirror as the Rider grew larger by the second. The truck was so old it didn't have the standard decal of newer models, but Ava was well aware of what they said and never were those simple words more terrifying:

Objects in the mirror are closer than they appear.

She tried not to scream, not to show just how petrified she was in this moment. She became aware of her heart thumping inside her chest. It pounded against her sternum like it was trying to escape. Like it knew that it was in danger. The rapid movement in her chest only served to scare Ava further. If, by some miracle, this piece of shit pickup truck could get them to safety, there was still the chance that Ava's heart could give out on her. Getting away wasn't necessarily a ticket to survival.

Her heart was beating so furiously inside her chest that she thought it would jump out of her body. She pressed her hand over it as if trying to keep it in place.

"Ava?" Jeremy's voice came from next to her, its typical concern overtaken by sheer panic.

"Jeremy," she replied, unsure of what she was going to say after.

"Is it your heart?"

"I'm... I'm... I'm fine." She tried to reassure him, but was starting to hyperventilate.

"Baby..."

Bobby turned sharply as the car came to a curve in the road, throwing Ava into Jeremy, who thrust his arms around her, doing his best to keep her steady.

"Is she okay?" he asked without taking his eyes off the road.

"No!" Jeremy shot back. "She's got a heart condition."

"A fucking heart condition?"

"I'm fine!" Ava spat out in between labored breaths.

"Too much exertion and she could go into cardiac arrest," Jeremy explained.

"Not for nothing, kid, but we don't have much of a choice right now."

Another curve. Another sharp turn. Ava slid into Jeremy, pushing him into the door as Bobby jerked the steering wheel. It rattled like it was going to pop open. Great. One more thing to be afraid of right now.

Ava stole another look in the side mirror. She couldn't see the Rider, but the sound of the bike was deafening. She forced herself to turn and look out the back.

The Rider was there. He was so close that he was practically in the cab with them. He was keeping pace with the inferior vehicle. It was obvious that he could overtake them, but he wasn't doing it. Not at the moment. What he was doing was staring. His face was still covered, but she could feel his eyes again and suddenly found herself transfixed. She wanted to turn back but couldn't.

Ava saw her terrified reflection in his goggles. It was clear as if she were looking in a mirror.

A mirror...

As soon as Ava made the connection, it happened. Her face seemed to swirl in the reflection and once again, she saw the girl. The one who was simultaneously her but not her. Her entire face was dripping with blood, running down from her scalp to her chin. A trickle turned to a gush before the face in the goggles burst into flames. Ava fell back against the dashboard and screamed as the sound of a blaring horn came from the front of the truck.

It wasn't Bobby's—as he skidded around the latest curve, a nondescript sedan swerved to avoid the truck which had invaded its lane. It narrowly missed colliding with them, but Ava's eyes tracked it as they drove past, watching it overcompensate as he swerved back to avoid driving off the road and barreling directly into the Rider.

Ava felt like she had just seen her favorite football team win the Super Bowl. The Rider's bike sparked as the sedan plowed into it, knocking him ten feet in the air and into the darkened woods.

"Oh, my God!" Ava exclaimed.

Bobby didn't take his foot of the gas. He maintained his speed as their unwitting savior got out of his car to examine the carnage.

"What are you doing? That guy may need help..." Ava said, not really thinking it through.

"We can't help him." Bobby said. "He's already dead."

Ava and Jeremy exchanged a glance. Now that the immediate threat of the Rider was past, it may be time to start wondering if their new friend here was crazy in his own right.

"Who are you guys?" Jeremy asked pointedly.

"Look, kid. I'll tell you the deal when we get to safety."

"Safety?" He responded. "Even if he survived that, I doubt he's walking away, let alone in any shape to get back on that chopper."

"You think so?" Bobby chuckled. "Let's hope you're right."

"You guys are some kind of motorcycle club," Ava interjected. "Like Hell's Angels, right?"

Bobby chuckled again. It was a wet chortling sound. He stroked his beard and held up his hand in disgust as something thick, wet and red dangled from his palm. He flicked his wrist to let the gore splatter on the seat next to him. Ava instinctively slid toward Jeremy, even though they were all covered in the stuff.

"Yeah, something like that. I'm sure you watch all the shows and know all about us though. So I don't really gotta explain it to you, I guess."

"Oh, we need an explanation, old man," Jeremy said.

"You ever shot a gun, Jason?"

Jeremy didn't bother to correct him. "Sure. A couple times."

Bobby stole a glance in the rearview mirror. Ava swiveled her head to confirm they weren't being followed. The highway behind them was empty and quiet. Too quiet.

"Open the glove box," Bobby instructed, nodding toward it.

Jeremy popped open the glove compartment and, lying there among discarded fast food wrappers and empty beer bottles was a handgun. Ava knew that Jeremy had a few friends who were really into hunting and sport shooting and he had gone with them a couple of times, but was by no means a sharpshooter or gun expert. She thought back to the old *Punisher Armory* comics she had seen among Jeremy's collection when he'd organized it a few months back. The Punisher was an ex-marine who fought a war on crime. The *Armory*_series wasn't so much a narrative, but rather a collection of splash pages with drawings of the Punisher's weaponry, along with a kind of diary explaining his thought process about each one. The gun he produced from Bobby's glove box looked familiar, like one of the ones in the comic, but she had no idea what kind of model it was. Or, more importantly, how to actually use it.

"Okay, its loaded, so keep that barrel pointed away from us."

Jeremy angled it toward the floor, holding it out from his body like it smelled bad or something. He made a conscious effort to keep his finger away from the trigger.

"Give it here."

Jeremy looked at the weapon in his hand and then at the blood-soaked ex-biker driving the cab. Bobby's hand was out and he curled his fingers toward him in a "gimme" gesture. Jeremy hesitated, wondering how smart it was to arm this dude.

Bobby noticed Jeremy's hesitation and rolled his eyes. "Kid, if I was going to hurt you, I wouldn't have told you about the damn gun, now would I?"

He and Ava locked eyes and had one of their silent conversations.

"For fuck's sake..."

Bobby's exasperation at the couple was interrupted by the sound of glass shattering. For the second time in less than an hour, Ava found herself covered in glass as air rushing in from the newly windowless rear of the cab washed over them. A roundish object thudded against the dashboard and bounced into Ava's lap. She looked down to see a mat of thick dark hair resting on her thighs. She turned the object and screamed as she held the severed head in her hands. It was that of a man, probably in his late thirties or early forties. He was clean-shaven and his mouth hung open in abject horror. His eyes were wide and lifeless, frozen forever in his final moments which, from the look of the ragged bloody stump of his neck, had been filled with fear and agony.

Ava dropped the head as if it had suddenly turned red hot. It rolled around the floor briefly before becoming wedged under the seat. Ava was both disgusted and relieved. It wasn't ideal to have it there, but better than it rolling around. She looked out the broken window and saw the Rider. It was as if he had been there the whole time. Somehow he had managed to get thrown from his bike and get back up without any visible injury, kill the poor soul that hit him and catch back up with them in time to throw the aforementioned poor soul's head through their window.

Was Bobby right? Was he some kind of ghost or demon?

It didn't matter. Whatever he was, they were all in immediate grave danger.

"Kid! The fucking gun! *Now!*"

Jeremy didn't hesitate this time. He handed the gun to Bobby, who immediately let it drop into his lap as he used both hands to turn around another curve. When the road went straight again, he took both hands off the steering wheel. He chambered a round, flicked off the safety, confirmed by the appearance of the small red dot.

Red, you're dead, he thought as he flipped the gun in his hand so that he was holding the barrel, and presented it to Jeremy who cautiously accepted it, looking down at the weapon in his hand, unsure of what came next.

"What the hell are you waiting for? Shoot that motherfucker!"

Jeremy turned and pointed the gun at the Rider. Ava saw his hands tremble. She couldn't blame him. He'd only shot bottles and paper targets before. Now they were in mortal danger and he was faced with shooting a person—at least, "person" would have to do for a description at the moment. She had her doubts. She saw a tear trickle down the side of his cheek.

"Shoot him, Baby!" she encouraged.

Her words were his motivation. He pulled the trigger and it exploded with a loud pop. It wasn't the overproduced bang of an action movie, but it was loud and every ambient sound from the motorcycle to the rattle of the truck suddenly sounded like it was under water. Her ears rang as she covered them in preparation for the next pop which came a second later. She heard Jeremy's muffled voice cry out.

"Fuck!"

She turned to see that the Rider was no longer behind them, even though the roar of the bike still grew louder. The Rider was now at their side. He stared through the window at her as their eyes locked again. They swerved around another curve and the Rider kept pace without ever looking away from Ava. It was impossible that he was riding this fast without looking at the road.

Jeremy fired again without thinking. The passenger window cracked and shattered as the bullet exploded through it. It missed.

"Damn it!" Jeremy shouted in desperation as he fired again.

The Rider slowed his vehicle just enough for the bullet to whizz by him. Ava expected that he would speed up, but instead he fell back, taking up position behind them again, but this time they were able to build some distance. Was he running out of steam? Were they about to catch a break?

Ava gasped as she watched him take his right hand off the grip and reach down on the side of his bike. She felt a lump in her throat as she knew what he was going for. He produced the machete, which glinted in the moonlight. He slowly raised it over his head, brandishing it like a Viking warrior wielding a battle-ax as he rode into battle. He cocked his arm back and Ava's eyes went wide.

"Jeremy! Shoot him! Now!" she screamed.

But it was too late. She saw his arm pitch forward and his fingers open as the blade left his grasp. It tumbled end over end in the air, almost in slow motion. Ava braced herself, expecting it to fly into the cab through the broken window, but she saw it lose altitude and sink below the truck bed. Thank God he'd missed. Or at least, so she thought.

Another pop came from beneath the truck. This time it wasn't the hollow, dry burst of gunfire; it was a sound like a very large balloon bursting.

Ava felt the truck shake as it found itself trying to move on only three tires. She saw the look of panic in Bobby's face that told his passengers he was no longer in control of the vehicle.

She heard the skid.

She heard Jeremy shout.

She heard the front of the vehicle crumple as they crashed into a pine tree for the second time today.

The sensations surrounding Ava were too numerous to fully take in. It was not surprising that Bobby's truck did not contain airbags, but it wasn't a welcome discovery all the same. Her head ached and she tasted coppery blood on her tongue. She hoped it was her own. Her head throbbed and without touching it, she could sense the egg that had quickly developed when she'd hit the dashboard. Everything sounded like it was submerged in water, but she didn't know if it was residual ringing from the gunshots and crash or if she was concussed. She felt groggy and out of sorts, focused more on assessing her current situation than worrying about the imminent danger they were still in.

She looked to her right and saw Jeremy grimacing in pain and holding his right shoulder, which hung limply at an odd angle, almost too low. It must have been dislocated. His face was sliced in multiple places, no doubt from the shattered window. It was hard to see just how many cuts there were as the blood mixed together to form a single crimson mask over half his face like that of a Batman villain.

"Baby!" she cried as she put her hand over his damaged arm. "How bad is it?"

"My shoulder," he moaned. "I can't get it back in place."

Ava had no clue how to pop a dislocated bone back into place. She felt around until she located the jutting protrusion and tried to be gentle but failed as Jeremy winced and cried out.

"I'm sorry!"

He thrust the right side of his body into the door. She wasn't sure if he was trying to put his bone back into place or if he was trying to push the door open. He wasn't successful in either endeavor and yelled again in agony. Still, he repeated the exercise again with a similar outcome.

Ava had forgotten they weren't alone in the vehicle. She turned to her left and saw Bobby slumped motionless over the steering wheel. Was he unconscious or dead? He had already been soaked in blood from the diner massacre when they'd got in the truck and it wasn't obvious what was his blood and what wasn't. She thought she saw him breathing, but if he was, it was shallow. Still, he wasn't her primary concern.

She turned and saw the Rider in the middle of the road about fifty yards behind them, sitting on his bike, watching the result of his handiwork. He wasn't moving for the moment, but she knew that wouldn't last.

"Shit! Jeremy, we have to get out of here now!"

Jeremy turned and saw what she was seeing. He immediately doubled his efforts, crashing into the door. Fuck the shoulder, he was trying to open the rusted, mangled door to get out. Ava leaned over him and tried to push on it, adding her own force to the effort. It was all useless. The door wasn't budging. They needed another way out.

Ava looked back again and saw the Rider had dismounted from his ride and was now standing next to it. It was like he was toying with them, gleaning some kind of sick amusement from their predicament, feeding off their fear.

She turned to Bobby. His large frame blocked them from climbing over and out of his exit. Ava was loath to touch him, but she didn't have much of a choice.

She grabbed and shook him as forcefully as she could, trying to rouse him, but, much like their efforts on the passenger door, was unsuccessful.

"Goddamn it!" she shouted in frustration.

"He's coming!" Jeremy warned.

Ava turned again and, sure enough, the Rider was slowly making his way toward the mangled vehicle. He wasn't in a hurry, knowing his quarry was trapped. Each step was deliberate. Almost savored.

Before Ava could contemplate what to do next, she saw Jeremy reach under his seat with his good arm. She cringed as she remembered what was under there and wondered what he was doing.

The answer revealed itself as she saw his arm jerk up as he thrust his body weight back, taking the seat with him. The maneuver allowed him to lift his legs up past the seat and over the dashboard. He pulled them back as if doing a crunch and then propelled them forward as hard as he could against the windshield. It was smashed up pretty good with cracks spiderwebbing all around it. New breaks formed around his shoes and the glass crackled and creaked under the force of impact. Ava turned back and saw the Rider continue his slow trek toward them.

"Hurry! He's coming!" she shouted as if Jeremy was somehow unaware of their predicament.

She didn't turn away, as she was transfixed by the madman's approach, but she heard the repeated cacophony of the windshield bending, but not breaking.

The Rider stopped just behind the truck bed.

"What do you want with us?" Ava screamed at him.

The Rider cocked his head looking at her. Ava felt tears well in her eyes as she understood that she had not posed the right question. Her voice cracked as she began to cry.

"What do you want with me?"

Jeremy's kicking beside her stopped momentarily. With everything they'd been through today, with every new weirdo they'd met, Ava seemed to be the common denominator. Whatever this was, it was about her.

"Tell me, you son of a bitch!" she screamed in an attempt at indignance.

Jeremy resumed his work on the glass. The Rider rolled his head back upright and stared for another long moment before he crouched down behind the pickup, only the top of his helmet visible.

The next impact beside her resulted in the loudest crack yet. Jeremy was making progress. She prayed that one more kick would open up the exit for them.

The Rider rose up from behind the truck's bed and yanked his arm back as he did. When it came up into view, it gripped the machete that had caused them to crash. It was caked with blood, both fresh and stale. He started around the passenger side.

"Jeremy!"

Her voice motivated him as he slammed his feet against the windshield and finally dislodged it, sending it crashing over the destroyed front of the vehicle. It teetered on the hood for a moment and then fell to the ground.

Jeremy used his good arm to help guide Ava through the newly formed exit. She crawled forward over the hood on her hands and knees and instinctively rolled off toward the driver's side, trying to put distance between the Rider and herself. She landed hard on the grass, but quickly rolled on her back so she could see if Jeremy was behind her.

He was doing his best, using his good arm to drag himself out. His torso was fully extricated from the wreck and he was working to pull the lower half of his body out when he suddenly jerked back. The Rider had him by the ankle and was drawing him back into the vehicle. Jeremy rolled onto his back and tried to kick his way out, but the Rider did not let go, his grip like iron.

Ava rushed around the tree to the passenger side, scouring the ground for a branch or piece of debris, anything she could use as a weapon, but found nothing. She had no idea how she was going to fight this guy without a weapon, but she couldn't just let him take Jeremy.

Her run abruptly stopped as she cleared the tree and saw the Rider pulling on Jeremy's leg with his left hand while brandishing his blade in his right. She saw first his ankle, then his calf emerge from the truck as the Rider yanked him out. He stopped once the lower half of his thigh was exposed and slowly raised the machete over his head.

"Hey!" Ava shouted, getting his attention.

The Rider paused and looked at the girl, forgetting about the victim in his hands.

"I'm right here, asshole! If you want me, come and get me!"

The Rider released Jeremy's leg and dropped his machete arm to his side as he turned to face her.

"Come on!" she screamed defiantly as she backed up back around the tree.

The Rider started toward her. Faster this time. More purposeful.

Ava turned to start running, but tripped over a jutting tree root. She crashed hard to the ground again. Her right knee burned as it scraped against the ragged bark. She grunted through the pain, but didn't wallow in it. She desperately pushed herself up on her hands and took off running down the road. She felt the wind against her face as she started moving at a speed she hadn't dared attempt since her diagnosis. She turned back to see if the Rider was still in pursuit. He was.

He was walking, but fast. Very fast. She knew if he went back and got his bike, she'd have no shot, but, for now, he was pursuing her on foot.

Ava felt the tightness build in her chest. It started to burn and her breathing became labored. She slowed despite her best efforts, but pushed forward. As long as he stayed on her tail, Jeremy was safe. She did her best to maintain the distance, but the Rider was rapidly closing the gap. Jeremy was out of immediate danger, but what was she going to do?

For now, she kept moving. She felt wetness building on her forehead, no doubt sweat mixing with the blood. She felt a sting as it dripped over her eye. She squinted hard and attempted to wipe it away with her forearm, only partially succeeding. She knew she couldn't keep this up much longer.

A now-familiar popping noise startled her. It came from behind her. She turned her head and saw the Rider had stopped moving. He stood in the middle of the road.

Ava took the moment to stop. At least to catch her breath. The Rider only stole a brief look at her before turning around. As he did, Ava noted a jagged hole in the skull that adorned the back of his vest. A red stream flowed down from it.

Another pop and this time she saw the Rider stumble backward.

Another.

Then another. Each sound pushing her assailant another step back.

One last pop and the Rider plummeted to the ground. He lost his weapon as his hand smacked against the pavement, the blade rattling briefly before coming to a rest.

She looked past him and saw Jeremy limping toward her, his good arm outstretched as it held the smoking gun. He pointed it down at the Rider as he approached.

"Ava?" he called out.

Ava dropped to her knees and let her arms fall limply over her thighs as she watched her husband approach. The Rider had not moved since he fell, but this was the same guy who got wrecked by a car and still managed to ride away. Maybe they were silver bullets or something.

Jeremy slowed his pace as he reached the Rider's body. He kept a wide berth, never lowering the gun as he sidestepped around him. When he reached the opposite side, he stayed focused on him and walked backward toward Ava. It was only when he reached her that he took his focus off the dead man. He dropped to his knees in front of her and she threw her arms around his neck, pulling him in close as she started to sob. Jeremy's right arm still hung useless at his side, but he pulled her in with his left, although he did not let go of the gun.

As the battered, weary couple embraced in the road, red and blue lights penetrated the darkness, followed by the wail of sirens. Ava's sobs intensified with relief. Help was finally here.

She lifted her head and saw behind Jeremy.

"No!"

Jeremy turned and pointed the gun in the direction she was looking.

The Rider was gone.

"What the fuck?" Jeremy exclaimed. "I hit him four times! Where the fuck is he?"

The lights and siren became more intense as two police cars skidded to a stop in front of them. Two uniformed officers jumped out of either side of each, guns drawn and pointed in the couple's direction.

"Drop the weapon!" one of the cops shouted.

In processing the shock of the Rider's disappearance, Jeremy must not have realized that he was still holding the gun. He quickly realized the foolishness of that decision and dropped it to the asphalt like a hot potato.

"Hands up!"

Ava complied and raised both arms over her head, fingers spread to make it obvious she wasn't holding anything. Jeremy raised his left arm in similar fashion.

He attempted to do the same with his right, but it just hung like a limp noodle.

One of the officers grasped a radio below his shoulder and clicked the button.

"Dispatch, Unit 214. Suspects in custody."

CHAPTER 7

Nooo...body knooows the trouble I've seen...

Ava laughed in spite of herself as the stupid cliched old song ran through her head. She sat on the cold metal bench in the holding cell at the police station, resting against the concrete wall, which was also cool and didn't exactly feel the worst pressed against her aching cranium. Her entire body was a jumble of pain and stiffness, but at least her heart rate had slowed.

She didn't fault the officers on the scene for treating them like suspects. They were covered in blood just a scant few miles from a diner that was littered with mutilated bodies of staff and patrons alike. Now having time to process what had actually happened in that eatery, she found it unlikely that she would step foot in a restaurant again any time soon.

The cops had cuffed them and read them their rights. One of the officers, a young man in his mid-twenties with a tightly faded hairstyle and a sorry attempt at a mustache, started to call for an ambulance, but Ava had stopped him.

"No! Take us to your station!"

The officers exchanged perplexed looks. She imagined it wasn't often that perpetrators would opt for a jail cell over a hospital bed, but Ava would rather be in a secure building filled with police officers than a medical facility where anyone could walk in or out.

"Are you refusing medical attention?" Mustache Cop asked.

"Yes!" Jeremy answered for her, seeing where she was going. "We need to get somewhere safe before he comes back!"

"That arm looks pretty bad," another, older, balder cop pointed out.

"He'll be fine!" Ava chimed in. "I'm sure you guys have a million questions about what went on back there and we'll answer every single one of them, but we need to get out of here right now!"

The cops hesitated for a moment, but the older officer noted that they could have EMTs meet them at the station. They put Bobby, who had regained consciousness just in time to be arrested, and Jeremy in one car and Ava in the other. The ride to the station was brief but silent. When they arrived, Ava was a bit dismayed at just how small the building was. It was only one story and not much bigger than her family doctor's office. And that was pretty damn small in its own right.

"This is your station?" she asked incredulously as Mustache Cop ushered her out of the vehicle.

"This ain't Trenton, ma'am."

Once she was inside, she felt a little better. The small office was staffed with about half a dozen officers and a receptionist who actually looked tougher than any of the rank and file there. They were printed, photographed and processed before being placed in the large holding cell in the back of the building. The older cop, whose name tag read "Sgt. Mahoney" told them he would be back to take statements shortly. Ava tugged on the bars, checking their sturdiness despite the unlikeliness that they could simply be pulled apart. The only view the cell afforded them was the walls around and a single, also barred, window that revealed nothing but moonlight. Ava didn't like not being able to see who was coming and going, but the room was as secure as any place they could have found themselves in this moment.

Jeremy winced in pain, holding his arm as he sat next to Ava on the bench.

Bobby nodded toward him. "You want me to fix that for you, Jason?"

"Jeremy," Ava corrected with more than a hint of an attitude.

"You want me to fix that for you, *Jeremy*?" He repeated, putting extra stank on his proper name.

"You expect me to believe you went to medical school?" Jeremy scoffed.

"I was a medic in Iraq, shithead."

Jeremy looked sheepish. He wasn't usually one to jump to conclusions about people and was ashamed he'd done so now.

"Patched up a lot worse injuries than some pussy-ass rich kid's boo-boo arm."

"I'm sorry..."

Bobby turned his back to him. "Yeah, I'll bet you are."

"How can you—"

Before he could answer, Bobby turned and grabbed Jeremy's wrist with his left hand. He thrust his palm against his shoulder and Ava heard a loud, hollow pop as the bone found itself unexpectedly back in place. Jeremy wailed in agony as Bobby offered a sly grin, clearly pleased with himself.

"What the hell is going on back there?" Sergeant Mahoney shouted.

"*Jeremy* here saw a spider," Bobby said. "He's a bit skittish."

Mahoney eyed them suspiciously, but only offered a "Keep it down" before going back about his business.

"Sorry, kid. Better you weren't anticipating it."

Jeremy exhaled sharp breaths filtered through gritted teeth as the pain became a memory.

Bobby took a seat on another bench across from the couple. He put his head down and fiddled with his hands, trying futilely to avoid eye contact and the interrogation that would no doubt follow.

"Who is he?" Ava demanded.

Bobby sniffed and spat in the corner of the cell. A gob of thick, brownish mucous smacked the floor before he wiped his beard with his sleeve. He met Ava's eyes, which repeated the question without actually saying it.

"His name is Caleb. Caleb Anders. We rode together back in the day."

"Hell's Horde?" Jeremy asked.

"Hell's Horde," Bobby repeated, somewhat wistful.

"What kind of shit were you into?" Jeremy asked with more than a hint of accusation.

"At first, nothing. Just a bunch of guys that liked to ride Harleys and drink beer. We weren't looking to be the Hell's Angels or nothing. Just a bunch of blue-collar guys, a few of us ex-military. Maybe one or two dust-ups with the law, but nothing serious."

"Was Caleb military?" Ava asked. "He seems like he's got some kind of training."

Bobby chuckled. "Naw. He wasn't military. Hell, wasn't anything all that special about him. Daddy was a blackjack dealer, if I remember right. Don't ever recall him talking much about his mom, so who knows what she was. Never held a job down for very long, just always managed to scrape by. If you're looking for someone that was the definition of average, that was Caleb."

"So how does average Joe, Caleb Anders, turn into the Terminator?" Jeremy asked.

"You know the worst thing about being average?" Bobby shot back.

Neither responded.

"The worst thing is that in a world where everyone is told they're special, that they can achieve their dreams if they stick their nose to the grindstone or some other such philosophical horseshit, being average makes you a fucking failure."

Bobby paused as if for questions, but the couple still remained silent.

"Caleb always wanted to be more. He could handle a Harley, but he wasn't the best. He pulled some tail, but never as much or as hot as some of the other guys. He was always just smack dab in the middle of the pack."

"I don't see how any of this is relevant," Ava said.

Bobby continued without acknowledging her. "Caleb was always sweet on this bartender working at The Well. You kids are too young to know it and, even if you weren't, you aren't exactly the typical clientele, if you catch my meaning. Her name was Vicki and she was drop-dead gorgeous. Every old outlaw in that place wanted a go-round with her, but no one—least to my knowledge—ever managed to seal the deal. So you can imagine our surprise when Caleb waltzed into our clubhouse one day with Vicki on his arm."

"So what?" Ava questioned. "She was playing him. Running some kind of scam which pissed him off and turned him into a psycho?"

"That what you do with men?" Bobby asked throwing a head nod toward Jeremy.

"Fuck you, dude," Jeremy said dismissively.

"I said keep it down!" Officer Mahoney's voice projected from down the hall.

Bobby glared at Jeremy. "Sit down and stop being so damn sensitive, kid. I'm just razzing you."

Jeremy slid back over to the bench with Ava. "Well excuse the shit out of me if I'm not in the mood for fucking jokes."

"Laugh so you don't cry, boy."

"So what's the point, Bobby?" Ava said, trying to get the conversation back on track.

"My point is that this gorgeous young thing that never showed any interest in any number of men that were better-looking, taller, better-built or better-hung than Caleb Anders was now inexplicably head-over-fucking-heels in love with him."

"Maybe women aren't as shallow as you think," Ava said.

"Oh, get off your high horse, honey," Bobby retorted. "It ain't like that. I'd been to that bar with Caleb a hundred and one times and, at no point did she show any interest. The boy was gaga over her and made no secret about it, but one day, out of the clear blue, she's dry humping him all over our club."

Ava and Jeremy exchanged glances again. The point eluding them.

"After Caleb hooked up with Vicki, he changed. Not in a bad way neither. He was more confident or something. Carried himself differently. When he talked, the guys started actually listening to him. I was in the service a long time and you can tell when someone's got, let's say, leadership qualities, but I've never seen anyone develop them overnight. But all of sudden, he was the most charismatic motherfucker in the room. He told a joke, everyone laughed. You had a problem, he had a solution."

"Wouldn't be the first guy to gain confidence by getting a girl out of his league," Ava said.

Jeremy grimaced even though he was fairly confident that wasn't a jab at him. Bobby snickered but didn't stop the story.

"It was a few months after he showed up with Vicki, that he started talking about 'expanding opportunities' for the M.C."

"What kind of opportunities?"

"The kind that would put more money in our pockets than we would likely make with the avenues available to us at the time."

"Illegal, I'm guessing?" Ava said.

Bobby shot her a look and then craned his neck trying to see down the hall. Ava got the hint. Probably best not to discuss your involvement in criminal activity in earshot of the police. He lowered his voice as he answered. "Started off small, mainly deliveries. Packages weren't big, but we didn't know what was in them. Drugs, I reckon."

"So, this guy Caleb bags a hot chick and becomes a crime lord?" Jeremy asked. The more Bobby explained, the less clear all this seemed.

"No. He wasn't calling the shots. He was working for some dude we only knew as Bill."

"You never met him?"

"Nope. Caleb was the only one who had contact with him."

"So how do you know he was real? That it wasn't Caleb running things?"

"Oh, he was real. The money that poured in once we started running jobs for him was very real. And there was a lot of it."

"What happened?"

"The jobs started getting more dangerous. Packages turned into crates. People started getting hurt."

"Killed?" Ava asked. Bobby didn't answer, but the look in his eyes did. Ava swallowed hard. "So the money justified it?"

"In our heads it did. We weren't exactly thinking straight, considering a lot of the cash went up our nose or down our gullets."

Jeremy got up and put his hands on the back of his neck, attempting to stretch as he addressed Bobby. "I still don't see how any of this adds up. What turned this dude into a motorcycle Michael Myers?"

"A job went bad. It was a pretty standard one, even the way things escalated. Details ain't really important. Had to escort a van full of some type of contraband across state lines, cops got involved, shots got fired. Some ended up dead. Some ended up getting pinched. Four of us got away. Me, Caleb, Eddie and Micah. We were smart enough to mask up and not wear our cuts so they couldn't pin anything on us no matter how much they suspected."

"I'm guessing Caleb wasn't happy about how things went down?"

"No. No he wasn't. Disappeared for over a week. When he came back, he was different again. He said Bill was pissed and that we needed to make it right or we'd all be dead. That's when it got well and truly fucked up."

"More fucked up than that?"

"We hopped on our bikes after dark that night. We rode a few miles toward the pines before he told us to stash our rides and follow him. He took us deep into the woods, to a beat-up old shack. I knew something was off. The whole thing felt like a setup. Eddie, Micah and I eyed each other and were ready to draw down on him if need be. He was outnumbered and we were on alert, so he wasn't going to get the drop on us."

"What was in the shack?"

Bobby paused. He looked upset. It was the first time his gruff exterior had cracked since they met him. He sniffed hard and answered.

"Vicki."

"His girl?"

"She was tied up and gagged. Buck naked. There were a bunch of weird-ass symbols all over her. At first, we thought they were drawn on, but they were cuts. The son of bitch carved a bunch of gibberish into that poor girl's skin."

"Jesus Christ," Jeremy muttered.

"He started ranting all this crazy shit. Bill had given him everything he wanted, including the girl of his dreams, but we fucked up his job and now we had to make a sacrifice. He was madly in love with that girl, but now all of a sudden he had her tied up, gagged and cut to shit. Now don't get me wrong, we all did some fucked-up shit back then, but ain't no way we were down with killing an innocent girl."

He spat again, as if trying to get a bad taste out of mouth. Ava noticed his eyes start to tear up as he continued.

"We told him we were leaving, but he put a machete up to Vicki's throat. He said we couldn't leave. Bill demanded a sacrifice or he'd kill us all. And not just kill us, but make us suffer. We hesitated and that was just enough time for him to slit her throat. He started chanting some nonsense as she bled out. It wasn't any language I knew. It was fucking insane and it was the last straw. Micah, Eddie and I pulled our guns and emptied our clips into him. I tried to stop Vicki from bleeding, but the bastard had cut her too deep. Was nothing I could do except watch her die."

"That's... horrible." Ava said. "What did you do?"

"Only thing we could. We cleaned up, took the bodies and buried them deep in the woods. We took Vicki a little further out. Didn't think it was the decent thing to bury her so close to the man that killed her."

"Did Bill ever track you down?"

"No," Bobby answered. "Been waiting for twenty years, but nothing happened until Micah was killed a few weeks back."

"Maybe that was how he made you suffer," Ava said.

"What do you mean?"

"You've been looking over your shoulder for two decades, waiting for someone to come try to kill you. Not my idea of a good time."

Bobby nodded. "Honey, you don't know the half of it. I've slept with a gun under my pillow every night since then. Every time I hear a bike rumbling down the road, my butthole tightens. I been waiting to die for two decades."

"So, what now?" Jeremy interjected. "The way I see it, this guy wants you. It doesn't have anything to do with us, so we should get as far away as possible from you."

"It's got plenty to do with you, kid."

Jeremy got up and walked over to the bars to attempt to get the cops' attention. "Excuse me! Officers!"

Bobby didn't say anything, instead, he reached into his shirt pocket and pulled out a folded photograph. He tossed it at Ava, but it landed a couple of feet in front of her. She leaned forward to pick it up and unfolded it, her eyes gaping in stunned horror as she looked at it.

"What?" Jeremy said as a tear fell down Ava's cheek.

The photo was an old Polaroid taken at what looked like a bar around which a group of bikers and their girls sat. She recognized a younger, thinner Bobby, and Eddie's head tattoos were unmistakable, but what really drew her eye was an average-looking guy seated with a shit-eating grin while a beautiful young brunette sat on his lap with her arms around his neck, flashing a smile at the camera.

It was the girl Ava saw in the diner mirror. The girl who looked exactly like her.

"That's Vicki," Bobby said.

Jeremy snatched the photo and looked at it in astonishment. He looked at Ava as if he'd never seen her before and needed to see if she was in fact the girl in the photo.

"Still think this has nothing to do with you?"

CHAPTER 8

A million thoughts assaulted Ava's mind as she tried to process the information she had just received. That girl, Vicki. Was it a coincidence? If so, it was a pretty fucking stunning one at that.

Ultimately, she guessed it didn't matter. If this Caleb nutjob thought she was his girl reincarnated, what difference did it make that she wasn't? The real pressing concern was what he intended to do with her. Was she destined for the same fate?

Her stomach churned and bile ascended her esophagus, taking all of Ava's willpower to keep from regurgitating.

"Babe?"

Jeremy's voice sounded miles away, but it was enough to draw her from her whirling confusion.

"Huh?" she responded dreamily.

Jeremy gave her a look as if to ask what she was thinking.

She looked to Bobby as she answered her husband's unspoken query. "This is all unbelievably messed up."

Jeremy turned his own focus toward Bobby. "So, this friend of yours survived the shooting."

Bobby scoffed. "Kid, we plugged him full of a dozen holes and tossed him in a pit in the deepest part of the woods. No fucking way he survived."

"Then how the hell do you explain everything that happened tonight?"

"Ain't on me to explain it. I just know shit's happening. And it's real bad."

"Very fucking helpful."

Ava grabbed Jeremy's arm and guided him back down onto the bench beside her.

"Forget it, Jeremy. He clearly can't help us."

Jeremy hunched over and rubbed his temples, favoring his injured arm as he did. Ava put an arm around him and rested her head on his shoulders.

"At least we're safe here."

The sentiment was hasty. No sooner did the word "here" leave her mouth than a thunderous crash echoed from the direction of the station's entrance.

What came next was a cacophony of chaos – screams, gunshots and the rumble of a motorcycle engine.

He was here.

At first, the gunshots were the sharp snap of pistols, but before long, they were overtaken by the unmistakable explosion of the shotgun. The one that had shattered their waitress's cranium.

The trio couldn't make out what was happening, but it became obvious that nothing the small police force were doing could slow down their enemy. Tears streamed down Ava's cheeks as she resigned herself to the fact that nothing was going to stop the Rider. Whatever his ill intent toward her, he would realize it tonight.

The cacophony of violence grew louder. Closer. The trio instinctively backed up as close as they could get to the wall, willing it to crumble and provide an avenue for escape. As Ava became aware of the jagged concrete pressing into the areas of raw, battered skin exposed by her minimalist choice of clothing, the sounds suddenly stopped.

It was little more than a moment, one saturated with tension, but, just as suddenly, the sound of footfalls on concrete broke the silence. They didn't sound right. The pace was hurried. The sound of the pursued, not the pursuer. She heard a metallic, jingling sound and her breath froze in her airway.

He had the keys. The bars could not save him.

The terror was short-lived as Officer Mahoney stepped out of the unknown void beyond the cell.

Blood covered him; Ava could not tell if it was his own. He held a large key ring in his left hand and his service weapon in his right: the same black handgun that he had drawn on them only a short time ago when he had taken them into custody.

"What's happening out there?" Jeremy asked.

Mahoney stammered a few unintelligible syllables as he started to fumble with the keys. His hands trembling beyond control.

"Is he here?"

"He... He..." Mahoney uttered.

"Just get us out of here. We can fucking chitchat later!" Bobby's voice boomed from the corner.

Mahoney stopped fighting the key ring and took a deep breath, understanding that he would not be able to get the cell open until he composed himself.

"Hurry!" Ava pleaded.

The rattled officer steadied his hand and finally managed to slide the key in.

Before he could complete the turn, a whistle cut through the air, followed by a metallic clang. Mahoney stopped cold as his eyes went wide. He turned his head to the left as Ava followed his gaze to see the machete, now all too familiar, caked with blood and indiscernible chunks, sticking out of the wall next to the right of the cell. It had spiraled too quickly to see, but the reality of what had just happened quickly became clear.

Mahoney let out a high-pitched wail as he gripped his forearm, pulling it away from the cell while his hand remained in place, gripping the key in the lock. A geyser of blood exploded from the severed limb as he tried to examine it, spraying his face in an almost comical manner, his scream turning to a gurgle as the viscous liquid filled his throat.

Ava heard another set of footsteps coming toward them. These were different. Heavy. Deliberate. Mahoney dropped to his knees, able only to continue wailing in terror and anguish as the footfalls loomed.

The Rider appeared, confirming the ownership of the thudding footsteps. He stopped in front of the devastated old cop on the ground in front of him. He looked down and cocked his head as Mahoney's screams became whimpers. Ava felt numb, like she was watching all of this from somewhere above.

The Rider turned to look at them. At her. His eyes remained obscured, but Ava felt that same burning gaze, but now it was even more intense. Was he seeing her or was he seeing Vicki? It didn't matter. She felt a chill down to her very soul. She wondered what he would do next.

She didn't have to wonder long. He reached down and cupped Mahoney's chin, tilting his head up. The move was almost gentle. It almost reminded her of Papa telling her it would be okay when she skinned her knee as a kid.

It wasn't okay.

The Rider intensified his grip and crudely raised Mahoney to his feet against his will, although he instinctively stayed there, his hand and his stump dropping to his side. The spray had subsided to a steady trickle and all color had drained from the injured officer's face, giving him the appearance of a living specter. He slumped against the Rider's chest, defeated like a boxer after a twelve-round pummeling. The Rider let him rest there for a moment before pushing him back upright.

He didn't give him a chance to fall back toward him. The Rider cocked his fist back before thrusting forward and caving in Mahoney's face. The sound of the impact was like a wet sack hitting a brick wall. Ava couldn't help but wonder if Mahoney would have screamed were he able, but he didn't really have a mouth anymore. Somehow he stayed on his feet, although the impact knocked him back. He stumbled and turned toward the cell, allowing the occupants a look at his ruined visage. His face and, by proxy, his skull had gone concave, a massacred mess of flesh and shattered bone. He was dead on his feet, but remained there for a few seconds before crumpling to the ground one final time. It should have been impossible to hit somebody that hard with a bare fist, but there was little doubt that this monster on the other side of the cage was no longer human.

The Rider stared down at the dead man on the ground, again admiring his handiwork, before turning to the trio he had cornered in the cell. His face remained obscured, but there was no doubt that Ava was his focus.

"What do you want with me?" Ava pleaded.

The Rider just stood in silence, continuing to stare. There was no noise from anywhere in the station. Ava had little hope that anyone in the building was still alive.

"What the fuck do you want?" Jeremy echoed angrily.

The Rider tilted his head briefly toward the angry young man, but almost immediately turned back to Ava. She felt her body go numb, almost as if she was entranced. She felt dizzy and the walls behind the psycho started to spin. She tried to move. Or at least she thought she did. None of her extremities seemed to obey her. She was frozen in terror.

The Rider grasped the metal bars of the cell and shook them. The three jumped in unison, each of them expecting the steel to give way, no matter how unlikely it seemed. Nothing that had occurred since this afternoon had followed any sort of logic. They flinched again as the Rider tried to yank the bars to the left, following the track to open to them. They rattled, the violent clanking sound eliminating their confidence that they would continue to hold. But they did hold, at least for the moment. The Rider continued to thrust, attempting to extricate his prey from their cage, but the bars managed to stay in place. He gave it one last pull before releasing them. He stood still, never taking his eyes off Ava, even though she could tell he was formulating his next move.

A sudden, sickening realization hit her like a ton of bricks. She did everything in her power not to turn her eyes toward Mahoney's corpse. She didn't even want to twitch her eyebrow for fear that it would somehow betray the idea that just popped into her head.

Whether it was some unknown tell or the Rider's own intuition, Ava was no longer the only one who had thought of a way in the cell.

Ava drew in a sharp breath as the Rider looked down at what was left of Mahoney. More specifically, the key ring that dangled from the dead man's belt.

Ava considered making a lunge for the keys. The body was sprawled close enough to the cell for her to reach them, but she was several feet away from him while the Rider stood directly over him. She had seen how fast he could move. Even if she could get the keys before he did, could she unhook them in time? What was to prevent him from grabbing her arm and ripping it clean from her torso?

She decided she had to try, but it was already too late. The Rider had the keys in his hand as soon as she'd taken her first step forward. The vision of the monster in possession of the only thing preventing him from getting to them froze her in her tracks.

"No!" she screamed as he inserted the first key into the lock. She expected it to open, but it didn't. He jiggled it a few times before removing it and letting it slide down the circular ring. He repeated the process with the next one. This one didn't work either. Still, this provided no relief to Ava or the others. There were only six keys on the ring and it was only a matter of seconds until the Rider would have unfettered access to them.

The third key jangled in the lock with no effect. The Rider showed no frustration, no emotion. With each failed attempt, he simply and methodically moved on to the next key.

The fifth key on the ring opened the lock. Ava felt herself throw up a bit in her mouth as the sound of the unlatching lock echoed in the empty hall. The Rider once again grasped the bars, this time with a single hand. The door offered no resistance as it slid open, leaving the trio completely exposed. Without taking his eyes off of them, the Rider reached his hand out toward the wall and dislodged the machete, letting it drop to his side. He took the first step into the cell.

Before the Rider could fully cross the threshold, a loud crack came from the other side of the hallway. Before they had a chance to identify the sound, chunks of the Rider's helmet shattered on both sides, with a spurt of blood spattering the wall to the left where, only moments ago, he had retrieved his weapon. He stumbled and fell atop Mahoney's body, losing the machete, which clanked to the ground beside him.

He didn't move. He wasn't breathing. He was dead.

It was over.

Ava was barely aware of what was happening around her. Right after the Rider was dropped, a group of police officers dressed in tactical gear rushed in to secure the scene. Their uniforms were different. She imagined these were state police. She wondered if there was even anything left of the local force. As much as she wanted to get out of this cage, she was also terrified of what they would see as they exited the building.

They instinctively put their hands in the air as the police swarmed in, but the rescuers treated them as victims, not suspects, ushering them out of the cell and down the hall. As they got to the edge, the apparent head of the unit, a large, gruff-looking African American cop stopped them at the door.

"We want to get you folks out of here, but you need to keep your heads down and eyes forward. There's things on the other side of this door that you don't want to see." He nodded toward Jeremy. "You. Put your arms on my shoulders and follow my lead."

He pointed at Ava and Bobby. "You two. Do the same with the person in front of you."

They did as they were told and got into position. Ava grabbed Jeremy's shoulders and Bobby did the same for her. Part of her was more than a little skeeved out at the thought of the old biker behind her like that, but on the spectrum of every fucked-up thing that had happened to them tonight, this was easily the least of them.

"You ready?"

Jeremy replied for the group. His voice cracking, nowhere near as assured as he wanted it to be. "Ready."

The door opened and the cop led them out. Ava did as he'd instructed. It wasn't a difficult order to follow. She had no interest in adding to the trauma they'd already experienced tonight. Despite their benefactor's best efforts, there was no way to completely shield them from what had happened. A wet, coppery odor assaulted her nostrils as they entered the main room of the station. It made her dizzy again, the scent throwing off her equilibrium. She stumbled, but managed to keep her grip on Jeremy's shoulders. She felt Bobby tighten his grip to keep from slipping and that nauseated her even more.

The cop stopped to let everyone regain balance. "You folks good?"

"Yes," Ava gasped, suddenly aware that her breathing was labored.

"Okay," the cop replied. "Almost there."

Ava felt panic rise in her stomach as her body started giving her warning signs. The dizziness. The nausea. The feelings were familiar. She felt her heart quicken.

Let's just get outside, she told herself. *Just get outside.*

They moved at a brisk pace through the room, relying on the cop to navigate them. Despite keeping her head down, there was no avoiding the blood on the floor. If this was the least traumatizing way out, she could only imagine how the rest of the place looked. She heard the front door open and felt a gush of still-hot night summer air wash over them; the smell faded as it was mixed with the heated asphalt of the parking lot. They followed the cop down the steps and into the lot. Once they had some distance, he spoke up.

"This is good here."

She looked up and quickly wrenched herself free from Bobby's grip, stepping forward next to Jeremy. The cop guided them over to a waiting ambulance which was parked with its lights flashing and door opened. There were a dozen police vehicles in the lot with twice as many emergency personnel. The moonlit sky was further illuminated with a blue and red glow from the lights of the vehicles.

Ava felt her breath catch in her throat. They were finally safe, but she felt a new panic. Her heart sped up faster as she tried to gasp for breath.

"Ava?" Jeremy's voice was both next to her and a mile away.

She clutched her chest as she felt it tighten, her shallow breaths becoming ragged.

"Ava!" Jeremy repeated. No longer a question, but an exclamation.

She fell forward, but Jeremy caught her, hooking her waist with his arm.

"What the hell's wrong with her?" Bobby asked.

"It's her heart! Help! Help!" he shouted in the direction of the ambulance as he pulled her toward it.

Ava saw the EMTs rushing toward her: a young woman with a short pixie hairstyle and full sleeve tattoos and a clean-cut guy in his thirties who looked like he spent every free moment in the gym.

She felt extra pairs of hands on her as Jeremy and the EMTs guided her onto a stretcher. Her eyes were open and she registered the woman's light shining in her eyes. The woman shouted codes or some such gibberish, but everything sounded further and further away as her vision coned. Jeremy's panicked voice tried in vain to keep her tethered to the waking world.

"Ava! Stay with me, baby! You hear me?"

She did hear him, but she couldn't stay with him. No matter how hard she tried. Jeremy's anguished cries were the last thing she heard as she slipped into darkness.

Chapter 9

Despite his exhaustion, Jeremy found himself pacing the ER's waiting room, the events of the past few hours spinning around his head like a lottery ball.

Ava's heart stopped when she collapsed, but the paramedics worked deftly and were able to resuscitate her reasonably quickly. When they had her as stable as possible, they hurried her into the ambulance. As they secured her, Jeremy attempted to climb in the back with her, but the cop who had assisted them in getting out of the station, Sergeant Robinson, grabbed his arm and kept him out.

"That's my wife!" Jeremy pleaded.

Robinson was not unsympathetic. "We'll follow her there."

Jeremy tried half-heartedly to wrench himself free, but he knew that it was neither a good idea, nor did it carry a likelihood of success.

"Listen, kid. I know the guy responsible for all this shit is the one lying in there with a hole in his head, but I gotta get you cleared, so if you get in the car and answer a few questions, we'll do that on the way to the hospital so you can be with your girl."

Jeremy nodded as he watched the ambulance peel out of the parking lot, lights flashing and siren blaring. He felt a pit in his stomach, wondering if he had seen his beautiful Ava alive for the last time.

He followed Sergeant Robinson's lead and got into the back of an unmarked squad car. Another uniformed officer was already behind the wheel, but he didn't even acknowledge him when he got in.

"You too," Robinson said, gesturing to Bobby. The old biker let out a heavy sigh, but otherwise didn't protest as he got into the back of the car with Jeremy.

Robinson explained that the cops knew that the Rider was the culprit behind the diner massacre and that Jeremy, Ava and Bobby were no longer under arrest. Jeremy wondered just what kind of evidence they had, but, being that the Rider was certainly not subtle, it wasn't a stretch to believe that he'd left a trail.

"You all have had one hell of a night," Robinson observed.

Jeremy recounted the whole story to the cops, leaving out the part about Bobby and his compatriots killing Caleb Anders years ago. He had no fucking clue how he would broach that one and, being that Bobby was unrestrained in the seat next to him, he figured it was best to gloss over that little detail.

Bobby, for his part, stayed silent as well, only confirming that he had encountered Jeremy and Ava in the diner and, being that they didn't have a car, helped them escape the massacre inside.

By the time they reached the hospital, the cop was convinced that he was transporting victims, not perpetrators.

"I'm letting you go, but once we get this shit cleaned up and sorted out, we're gonna want to talk to you again." He eyed Bobby less sympathetically before adding, "Both of you."

Bobby gave him a sarcastic salute. "Whatever you say, chief."

It had now been about forty-five minutes since they'd arrived. Bobby was outside smoking while Jeremy anxiously awaited an update on Ava's condition. The receptionist had looked at him sideways when he first rushed up to the desk. He hadn't even considered how rough he looked. She asked if he needed medical attention. Even though he almost certainly did, he refused, stating that he just wanted to know about Ava. The receptionist confirmed that she was inside, but had no other updates and encouraged him to have a seat.

He sat for all of thirty seconds before he felt the need to move. The adrenaline was draining and he was definitely aware of the pain that wracked his body, but his anxiousness about his wife's condition kept him from remaining sedentary.

The phone at the receptionist's desk rang and, for the first time in several hours, Jeremy realized that he didn't have one. Then it hit him. Ava's parents. She always dutifully called them when they returned from a trip, no matter how briefly. They'd been expected home that afternoon and it was now just past midnight. They must be beside themselves with worry, maybe even in a full-blown panic at this point. He looked at the closed doors leading back to the emergency room bays and contemplated asking the receptionist to use the phone so he can confirm to Ava's parents that their worst fears were indeed being realized.

As he was weighing his course of action, a voice behind him startled him. "Any word on your girl, kid?"

It was Bobby, cigarette smoke clinging to his clothes as he re-entered the waiting room.

Jeremy shook his head, dejected. "Not yet."

Bobby plopped himself into the nearest chair and folded his hands over his sizable stomach, looking a bit too relaxed given what they'd just been through.

"I gotta call Ava's parents," Jeremy said, more to himself than his unlikely companion.

"Where you kids from?"

"North," Jeremy answered, thinking it better to leave out specifics.

"You should probably wait till you talk to the doc. No sense getting them panicked until you know there's something to panic about."

"They're already panicked. They just don't know how much they should be yet."

"Do as you will, kid. Just my two cents."

Jeremy mulled it over for another moment, but ultimately decided it was better to rip the Band-Aid off and tell them now. Not that he really knew how he was going to say it.

He made his way over to the receptionist. "Excuse me..." he started.

Before he could officially make the request, the door to the back of the ER buzzed and a tall, gangly man with a thin wisp of a mustache, clad in blue scrubs and a white lab coat, came out.

"Mr. Allegretti?"

"Yeah," Jeremy answered eagerly not bothering to correct the doc on his last name.

"Have a seat," the doctor said, gesturing to the chairs.

Jeremy did as he asked, resting on the edge of the seat, leaning forward to hear what the doctor had to say.

"I'm Dr. Schaefer," he said. "Your wife went into cardiac arrest in the ambulance. They were able to resuscitate her within a couple of minutes, so she likely avoided dire complications like losing oxygen to her brain, but she's not out of the woods. She's in critical but stable condition at the moment."

Jeremy exhaled, not realizing he had been holding his breath, as the doctor continued.

"However, her heart rhythm is very unstable. We've been trying to get it under control with lidocaine, but it keeps elevating despite our best efforts."

"What does that mean?" Jeremy said, feeling the panic settle in his throat, cracking his voice. "What can you do?"

"That depends. We don't have any medical records on her. Are you aware of an existing heart condition?"

"Yes. She has something called ARVD. I don't remember exactly what the letters stand for."

"Arrhythmogenic right ventricular dysplasia," Dr. Schaefer said without skipping a beat. "That explains what's happening."

"So what can you do?" Jeremy asked, more urgently this time.

"We're going to have perform a procedure known as an ablation," the doctor replied.

"The fuck is that?" Bobby asked.

"Who are you?" the doctor asked.

"I'm his accountant," Bobby said nodding toward Jeremy.

The doctor ignored him and continued addressing Jeremy. "An ablation is where we go in with a catheter and burn away the scar tissue, which will hopefully put the heart back into rhythm."

"Jesus!" Jeremy exclaimed. "How dangerous is that?"

"Typically it would be a relatively safe procedure, but unfortunately this is not a typical situation."

"Why not?"

"We do these on stable patients, not ones that are in active cardiac distress."

"Can you stabilize her first?"

"If we could, we would, but we need to do this right away or we could lose her."

Jeremy stared unblinking at the physician as a single tear fell out of his eye and down his cheek as the doctor continued.

"I'll need you to sign a form giving us permission to proceed as her next of kin."

Jeremy couldn't find the words to verbalize his agreement so he simply nodded. The doctor stood up and motioned for Jeremy to join him while simultaneously giving Bobby a look that instructed him to stay put.

"There's one other thing you need to be aware of."

"What?"

"This is already a precarious situation to be performing this procedure, but there's also a risk to the child, especially in this early stage."

The word hit Jeremy like a freight train. He had to repeat them to make sure he heard them right.

"Child? Ava's... she's... pregnant?"

Dr. Schaefer realized that this was news to the young man and offered him a sympathetic glance. "You didn't know. I take it this was not a planned pregnancy?"

"She... she didn't want to have... She was afraid with her condition..."

"I see," the doctor responded. "We'll do everything we can to keep them both safe, but we have to move now to get her prepped for the procedure. Do you understand?"

Jeremy nodded again. "How far along is she?"

"Tough to say at the moment. Probably about five or six weeks."

Five or six weeks. Ava hadn't mentioned anything about missing a period, but then that wasn't unusual. Since her diagnosis, her menstrual cycles had been irregular at best, even giving the couple a scare or two early on in their relationship although they took reasonable precautions. Admittedly, they could let their desire trump caution at times.

Jeremy's stomach churned as he found himself facing the realization that there was now more than just his wife in danger. His future family was about to be placed in the hands of this medical team.

Assuming she made it through the procedure okay, Jeremy wondered how Ava would react to the news. Would she embrace the idea? Would she want to try to carry through with the pregnancy. Would they end up with the two-story house with the white picket fence? Would it be a boy or a girl? Would they play sports? Would they look like their mom or dad? So many questions, so much uncertainty hitting all at once. It was almost too much to take. He felt faint, but managed to maintain his composure as he quickly scribbled his signature on a number of different forms that he didn't bother to read.

Once he'd finished, the doctor told him that they'd get her prepped and into surgery right away.

"Can I see her?" Jeremy asked.

The doctor was hesitant, but nodded. "You'll have to be quick, but we'll give you a few moments before we take her back. Follow me."

Jeremy did as instructed. Dr. Schaefer waved the white card hanging on the lanyard around his neck against a black sensor to the right of the emergency room doors, opening up access to the back. He led Jeremy to a small bay with the curtains drawn closed. He stopped him before he could make his way inside.

"I'll give you two minutes. She's sedated, so you can talk to her, but don't expect a response."

"Can she hear me?" Jeremy asked.

"Possibly. But she may not remember if she does. Sedation is a tricky thing. Everyone reacts to it differently."

"Thank you," Jeremy said somberly before pushing his way between the curtains. The pit in his stomach tightened as he saw the love of his life lying unconscious in the bed, an oxygen mask affixed over her mouth and nose. Her bloody, dirty clothes lay in a pile on the chair in the corner of the room, leaving her clad in only a hospital gown. An intravenous tube protruded from her arm, leading to the clear bag hanging from a pole with who knows what type of medication pumping into her. A blood pressure cuff whirred as it tightened around her forearm, registering its latest reading.

Jeremy walked over and gently took her limp hand in his own, more tears materializing from his ducts as he did.

"I should have taken you somewhere nicer than Atlantic City," he said, half-joking, half-lamenting. "Please fight this, baby. You're so strong. You never let this condition define you; don't let it take you now.

We have so much life to live. You, me and our child. I know you thought you couldn't do it. I know you're scared. I'm scared too. But I know if you can come out on the other side of this, we've won. We've fought so hard today to survive. I know you're tired, but please, please, please. Just fight a little longer. Then we can go home and be a family."

He squeezed her hand, hoping in vain that he would feel the pressure of her grip in return. He didn't.

"I love you so much, Ava. I'll see you when you wake up."

Jeremy was a little surprised to find Bobby still in the waiting room when he returned.

"How is she, kid?" Bobby asked with seemingly genuine concern.

Jeremy sat across from him and slumped in the chair, the adrenaline no longer able to hold back his exhaustion. He felt a twinge of pain in his shoulder, gritting his teeth while trying not to grimace. He didn't know why, but he didn't want to show weakness in front of the old biker.

"She... she looks so..."

He dropped his head into his hands brushing his hair back as he did. He wasn't crying, but the words weren't coming either.

"It ain't easy to see someone you love like that. I get it."

Jeremy looked up and met Bobby's eyes. "They're bringing her back for surgery."

"Then she's got a shot. All you can ask for."

"All I could ask for was that none of this bullshit happened."

"Can't change the past."

Jeremy's expression hardened. "Why are you still here?"

"Fuck if I know," Bobby replied. "I go to grab a burger at the diner tonight and all hell breaks loose, ended up with the two of you in my truck, then the three of us in jail. Figure I might as well stick it out with you to make sure she's okay."

"Why? You've already done more than enough."

Bobby chuckled, eliciting a wet cough. Jeremy softened a bit, understanding that he wasn't the only one banged up from the evening's events.

"Kid, I couldn't get you away fast enough for him not to catch us, I couldn't stop him from coming after us in the jail and I damn sure couldn't help Vicki when she passed out."

Jeremy raised an eyebrow. "Ava."

It took a second for Bobby to realize his mistake, mumbling a staccato apology. "Shit. Sorry kid. Of course. Ava."

Jeremy nodded and the two sat in silence for a bit. The waiting room was empty other than the two of them and the receptionist separated from them by a wall with a glass partition. A television mounted in the corner played one of those home improvement shows. The ones where a family of five on a philosophy teacher's salary somehow had a $1.5-million budget to buy and renovate a house in the richest section of town. The volume was down or broken, so there was no sound to cut through the uncomfortable silence.

Jeremy kept glancing toward the door, knowing that it was too soon for news on Ava's condition. The doctor had said the procedure might take between two and four hours. Glancing at the clock on the wall, it had only been twenty minutes since she went back. If the doctor emerged from behind the door right now, he would no doubt come bearing bad news. He turned to Bobby, who was occupying himself with a copy of *Good Housekeeping* magazine.

"Why does she look like her?"

Bobby looked up from the magazine.

"Vicki," Jeremy repeated. "How does she look like her? They could be twins."

"I don't know. Damnedest thing I ever saw."

There was a line of inquiry Jeremy contemplated entering into. He couldn't believe he was going to go there, but this night was so fucked up that a little more crazy in his life really wouldn't make a difference.

"When this guy Caleb started coming around with Vicki, you said he changed. Like he was a different person overnight."

"Yeah. That's right."

"So, could it have been more than just a shot of confidence?"

Bobby cocked an eyebrow at him.

"Meaning?"

"Meaning, was it something... supernatural?

"Like ghosts and shit?"

"Dude, according to you, a guy you killed twenty years ago has been after us all fucking night and now you don't believe in ghosts?"

"Kid, I don't know what the fuck I believe. I can't wrap my head around this shit. My buddy Micah got his fucking head chopped off a few weeks ago and now I saw a guy I thought was buried out in the woods. I'm not exactly an expert in this shit."

"What about the sacrifice? That's what you said, right? Caleb carved a bunch of symbols into his girl and then cut her throat. Were they... satanic?"

"How the fuck should I know?" Bobby snapped.

"You never saw anything like that before?"

"What are you trying to say? That all us bikers worship the devil or some shit. Boy, that's downright ignorant."

"C'mon, man, I'm not accusing you of anything. I'm just asking you about what you told us."

Bobby took a deep breath, composing himself. "Yeah. It was weird, okay? I never got into any of that Satan shit, but those symbols, the nonsense he was chanting. It was something dark and sinister and it still chills me to the bone thinking about it to this day. I did some shit, kid. Shit I'm not proud of and I know I'm going to get what's coming to me, but I never wanted anything like what happened in that shack that night."

Jeremy toned his voice down, trying to find sympathy. After all, for whatever he was or whatever he'd done in the past, Bobby had saved their lives tonight. And he was still here with them. Regardless of the circumstances that led up to their meeting, they were now in this together. Rather than continue pressing him on something that he clearly didn't fully understand either, Jeremy simply looked him in the eyes and said: "Thank you."

Bobby gave him a look as if to say *For what?*

"Thank you for everything you've done tonight. We wouldn't have made it without you."

Bobby met his gaze, pursing his lips as if trying to avoid matching the sentiment. He nodded in acknowledgment as the two men went back to sitting in silence, knowing there was nothing to do at this point but wait. Wait and pray.

CHAPTER 10

Broiling hate bubbled up from the pit of the Rider's stomach as he regained consciousness. His awareness was the first thing to return. Although his limbs did not respond right away, he could feel that he was lying flat in a moving vehicle, the bumps of the uneven road jostling his limp body as he lay prone.

He was also aware of a sense of confinement along with the fetid stench of plastic mixed with blood. He opened his eyes and saw nothing but black, blinking a few times to clear any possible obstructions diluting his vision, although there were none. He was also aware that he was no longer wearing a helmet; the back of his head rested on something resembling a cot that he could feel through his plastic encasement.

For a few minutes, all he could hear was the soft hum of the vehicle's engine punctuated by the occasional thud of a particularly pronounced bump in the road. The silence was broken eventually by a muffled, male voice.

"You hungry?"

A raspy female voice responded. "I'm always hungry, Doug."

"You want to grab something after we dump this dude at the morgue?"

"Yeah. I'd love to get some pancakes at Lola's, but," her voice lowered to a mutter, "Jesus Christ."

"Yeah," Doug replied. "Poor Courtney. Such a sweet kid. Can't believe this bastard did that to those people. We should just toss him in the goddamn Atlantic and call it a day.

"Can't let emotion be part of this job, Dougie. You know that."

"Yeah, well this is my first mass murderer, so you'll have to excuse me if my professionalism is slipping."

"You said a mouthful. Creeps me out just having him back here."

They fell silent for a few minutes. The Rider could feel his extremities, but he did not yet have control. While he moved, the voices returned.

"How's Alice feeling?" the female asked.

"She's weak. Tossing her cookies just about every hour. The chemo's really doing a number on her."

"I'm sorry, Doug. How many more treatments does she have?"

"Four. Then they do another scan."

"You know, you can take some time off."

"I know, but we need the money and the night shift pays better. The insurance covers some, but nowhere near enough. I almost missed the mortgage payment last month. Managed to scrape together the last of it right on the fifteenth."

The Rider felt his finger move. Just a bit as the female voice chimed back in. "You got someone staying with her and the girls while you're at work?"

"Her mom is there tonight. So, I get off at six, home by six thirty, which means I'll be catching an earful of shit by six thirty-five."

The female laughed. "Doris still hasn't warmed up to you?"

"That woman wouldn't warm up if I set her couch on fire with her on it."

Another laugh from the woman. "Don't get any ideas."

The Rider tried to move again. He felt his entire arm lift.

"What the hell?" Doug exclaimed.

"What?" The female asked.

"I think he just moved."

"Moved?"

"Yeah, the fucking bag moved!"

"It was probably that pothole we hit. Stop being a baby."

Silence again. The Rider, though aware of the conversation, was not particularly interested in the content. He went about trying to move again, seemingly without success.

"Jesus Christ!" Doug shouted.

"Holy shit, what now?" the female asked, sounding decidedly irritated.

"He definitely just moved. I saw his arm lift up."

"You need some coffee or something, dude. The guy caught a bullet through his skull. He's dead as a goddamn doornail."

"I'm opening the bag up and checking."

"If it makes you feel better, go for it."

The Rider heard the sound of a zipper and, without warning, light flooded the darkness as he found his confinement released.

A scrawny, middle-aged man with a long, drawn face and heavy bags under his eyes, obviously Doug, came into view. The Rider remained motionless as the man examined him through narrowed eyes. He saw the curiosity in the man's features twist into revulsion as he did.

"Fuck," Doug whispered, but not so low as to avoid detection by the woman.

"What?"

"I forgot just how fucked up this guy actually is. His face looks... rotted."

"So?"

"So, it's like he's been dead a long time."

"Well, considering he just got shot an hour ago, I think your forensic analysis may be a tad off."

Doug, backed out of the Rider's field of vision. "Look at him."

"I don't need to look at him. I saw him when we bagged him. That was enough for me."

Doug slowly re-entered the Rider's field of vision. His nose wrinkled as he looked over the "corpse."

"Holy hell."

"What now?" the woman's voice bristled from the distance.

"Shit, Dani," Doug said as he narrowed his eyes. "It feels like he's looking at me."

"For fuck's sake, Doug, zip him back up so you stop freaking yourself out. You've barely slept in weeks. You're probably damn near hallucinating at this point. Seriously, man, you need to take some time off to be with Alice."

Doug took a few long moments trying to determine if there was any awareness behind the Rider's eyes, no matter how implausible it seemed. He let out a long, protracted sigh, as if trying to reset his mind.

"Fine," he muttered as the Rider heard the sound of the zipper slowly moving back.

As the darkness crept back in, all the Rider's senses returned in an instant. Doug emitted a shrill wail devoid of any masculine characteristics as the dead man sprang up on the gurney, the plastic of the body bag splitting apart as he rose. The Rider turned his head to the petrified paramedic, showing him that there was no question that there was awareness in his eyes.

The Rider felt himself jolt to the left as the ambulance swerved, Dani spewing puzzled expletives as she tried to control the vehicle.

A second swerve sent the Rider back into Doug's direction and he used the momentum to grab the panicked man's throat, turning his most recent scream into a choked gurgle. The Rider pulled Doug with him as the ambulance swerved once again in the other direction. He felt his fingers sink into the man's flesh. He felt wetness before he saw the blood leaking out around his digits. He felt a rush of euphoria while he squeezed his hand shut, taking a chunk of flesh from the medic's throat. He tore it away, causing an explosion of blood to paint the back of the ambulance as Doug crashed back in the opposite direction. He tried to cry out, his ruined neck making the effort impossible.

The ambulance swerved one more time before the Rider was jostled again by the ambulance coming to a sudden screeching halt as the driver jammed on the brakes.

"Doug!" the woman shouted. "What was that? What's happening?"

The Rider looked at the chunk of flesh resting in his bloody hand before turning his attention back to Doug. He was still alive, albeit barely. He had given up on covering his wound, his hands resting at his sides. His eyes were rolled back into his head and he made breathing-type motions even though he could not take in any air. The blood flow had already morphed from a gush to a trickle. The Rider knew the man would not survive, but he wanted to inflict more harm before he perished. As he slid the rest of his body out of the body bag he heard a click in front of him.

The night sky was lightening as dawn approached. The air, already humid, smacked him in his face, the sensation feeling different with his face now exposed. Dani, a heavyset woman in her late thirties with thick glasses and a tight ponytail, screamed at the sight of her dying colleague. She turned to run, but tripped over some unseen obstacle and hit the ground hard, her glasses skidding away from her.

As she tried to crawl away, the Rider got to his feet and made his way out the back of the ambulance. She moved as fast as she could, but even at a walking pace, the Rider was faster. As soon as he was close enough he grabbed her ponytail and yanked her entire body violently backward, her head cracking against the pavement as she fell. A whimper escaped her lips, the sass in her voice from her banter with Doug completely gone. The Rider stood over her and bent over, grabbing both sides of her head, lifting her up until she was inches from his ruined face.

She screamed and let out a final plea. "Please... don't... I have a baby."

Whether that was true or some kind of last-ditch effort to garner sympathy didn't matter. Her words turned back into screams as the Rider jammed his thumbs into her eyes, crushing them deep into her skull. He pressed down as far as he could before he closed his hands into fists inside the woman's head. With one deft movement he twisted her head entirely around and dropped her to the pavement, her face slapping against it with a wet thunk.

The Rider examined his victim, certain she was dead, but he decided to put an exclamation point on the matter. He raised his foot over her head and held it for a moment before slamming it down as hard as he could, crushing her skull like a melon. The Rider savored the moment, his rage momentarily satiated by his brutality. Finally, he lifted his foot out of the husk that used to be Dani the paramedic, slimy gore dripping off the steel toes of his boot. He looked back toward the ambulance and saw that Doug had fallen over, almost certainly dead. He thought for a moment about inflicting more damage on the corpse, but he had other things to do.

As the sun began to peek out over the horizon, the Rider made his way down the road.

Chapter 11

Jeremy woke up in a chair, shutting his eyes as soon as they opened. Sunlight was flooding into the room, practically blinding him. It had still been night the last he recalled. Exhaustion must have finally overtaken him because now the full morning sun hovered high in the sky.

Something felt wrong. Jeremy couldn't exactly put his finger on it, but the air in the waiting room felt heavy and oppressive. As Han Solo would say, he had a bad feeling about this. It felt like she had been in surgery for hours, but time had slowed to a crawl, the universe playing the cruel joke of making the last twenty-four hours feel interminably long despite how much had occurred. He alternated between sitting with his leg bouncing so fast he felt like it would burst through the floor like a jackhammer, and getting up and pacing laps around the room. His mind alternated between confusion, fear and bewilderment. Ava was alive, but in danger. She was pregnant but didn't know it. Not to mention the fact that they had almost been killed a dozen times over since that afternoon.

"Kid."

Bobby's voice startled him.

"Huh?" he asked in a daze.

"Come on outside with me."

"Why?"

"Trust me."

That was a weird concept. A scraggly old biker that he had only met a few hours back during a mass murder was telling Jeremy to "trust him." But he'd saved their lives, no doubt about that. And he had shed light on why this was happening, even if it was still impossible to grasp.

"What if the doctor comes out?"

Bobby looked over him to the receptionist. "Miss?"

The woman behind the desk looked up.

"My colleague and I are gonna step outside for a moment. Can you let the doc know where we are if he comes out?"

She looked back down at her phone, muttering a barely audible, "Sure."

"C'mon kid."

Jeremy followed Bobby outside and off to the side of the entrance. Bobby leaned against the brick exterior of the building with a sigh as he reached into his shirt pocket and fumbled around for a moment. When he removed it, he was holding a crumpled joint and a single match between his fingers.

"What the hell is that?" Jeremy asked even though he knew damn well what it was.

"What do you think?" Bobby said as he struck the match against the wall, quickly bringing the flame to the tip and lighting it. The smell was potent and hit Jeremy's nose immediately. He recoiled a bit, more from the surprise than an aversion to marijuana, a drug he occasionally partook in himself. Bobby exhaled a plume of smoke and flipped the joint in his fingers, pushing it toward Jeremy.

"Figure you could use a little mellowing out."

"How did they not confiscate that at the jail?"

Bobby laughed. "They thought they had us for multiple homicides. They weren't exactly concerned if we had weed on us."

He thrust the smoking joint a bit more toward Jeremy. He hesitated for a moment, but took it and examined it, not even sure what he was looking for.

"I ain't got cooties if that's what you're thinking."

Jeremy laughed in spite of himself. Bobby was crude and their situation was more than a little fucked up, but there was something endearing about the guy. Maybe they were just bonded through the trauma which helped him overlook the fact that he was essentially a criminal. Whatever the case, Jeremy had learned tonight that there were worse monsters out there than this guy.

He took a deep drag off the joint and coughed as he exhaled. It had been a while.

Bobby chuckled again. "Not like that schwag you college kids get, is it?"

Jeremy smirked and took another drag. He felt like he was going to start coughing again, but managed to suppress it, mainly to prove that he could handle it. He tried to be casual as he passed it back and laughed in spite of himself.

"What?" he asked.

"I done lots of shit in my time. Most of it revolved around bikes, broads and booze. Now here I am smoking reefer outside a clinic with an uptight rich kid whose girl just had surgery after an attack by a dead friend of mine. Life sure is fucking funny, ain't it?"

He laughed harder, the thought hitting him in the funny bone just the right way.

Jeremy chuckled too. "Legal or not, I'm pretty sure we aren't supposed to be doing this out here."

Bobby took another hit and added, "Well, worst they can do is tell us to put it out. Kid, you just beat a murder rap. Breaking a few non-smoking rules isn't the end of the world."

"Shit," Jeremy muttered under his breath. The gravity of what could have happened to them if they'd been charged with murder hitting him around the same time as the weed. "We could have all gone to jail for the rest of our lives."

"No shit," Bobby replied. "Good thing we didn't. I'm too pretty for prison."

They both started laughing now, the combination of marijuana and exhaustion sending them into delirium.

While they were lost in the moment, the doors opened and Dr. Schaefer stepped out. Bobby quickly passed the joint to Jeremy, who took it without thinking, although as soon as he realized he was holding it, he quickly tossed it over his shoulder as if the doc wouldn't notice. His breath was barricaded in his chest, rendering him unable to speak. His eyes had to do the talking, silently asking the physician his burning question about Ava's condition because his words could not.

"She did well," Dr. Schaefer said. "The procedure went smoothly and she's in recovery now."

Jeremy exhaled, an action that was a bit painful due to his injuries, exacerbated by the marijuana. He had been so concerned for Ava's health and safety that he hadn't really stopped to think about all the trauma his own body had suffered. Between the car crash, his shoulder injury and almost non-stop running for his life, he wasn't exactly in peak physical condition at the moment. Still, his relief at hearing that Ava was okay outweighed any discomfort.

"Thank you so much, doc," he exclaimed, a little louder than he intended.

Dr. Schaefer gave him a measured look.

"She's stable, but she's not out of the woods yet," he explained. "I don't know all the details of what you both went through tonight, but there's been a tremendous physical strain on her heart. With someone in her condition, it's difficult to tell what, if any, long term effects she may experience."

Jeremy swallowed hard, a lump forming in his throat. "And... the baby?"

Dr. Schaefer gave a reassuring nod. "The baby is fine as far as we can tell, but I recommend she make an appointment with her ob-gyn soon."

"How long until we can go home?"

"We need to observe her for the next twenty-four hours. If she remains stable, we can release her pending a follow-up with her cardiologist."

"Can I see her?"

The doc gave Bobby the side-eye again. "Just you."

Bobby put his hands up in an *I didn't do nuthin'* gesture. "All good with me, doc. I gotta recover my own medicine that Polly Paranoid here just tossed away 'cause he forgot it ain't illegal no more."

Schaefer frowned, unamused. "Let me call up to the nurse to see if she's awake yet. If so, we'll have someone bring you up."

Jeremy extended his hand and the doctor accepted and shook it.

"Thank you, Dr. Schaefer. Thank you so much."

Dr. Schaefer nodded in acknowledgment and turned to go back inside.

Jeremy leaned against the wall and sighed in relief as Bobby pushed aside the bushes to try to find his joint.

"Goddamn it, Jimmy, you threw it in a damn puddle!"

"You seriously still don't know my name?"

Bobby snickered. "Just fucking with you kid. Go check on your girl."

Chapter 12

Grady hated the night shift. You'd think from watching movies that all the cool shit at the impound yard would happen at night, but it wasn't even close. All he saw was the cops bringing in cars confiscated during DUI busts.

Tonight was a little different, though. A little after 1 a.m. they brought in a sweet-looking motorcycle. Grady had never ridden one and couldn't tell you the difference between a Harley and a Honda, but he knew there was something about this one. It emanated a kind of energy. Something Grady could feel as the tow truck pulled up to his booth.

Lester had stepped out of the truck's cab. He was tall and skinny, with long hair tied back in a ponytail and a wispy chin goatee. Grady was short, stout and clean-shaven, his combover not fooling anybody. The two were polar opposites. Lester made his way to Grady who managed one last bite of his hoagie, lettuce and onions spilling out the opposite end and plopping onto his desk.

"Whatcha got, Lester?" Grady asked, the words muffled as he multitasked chewing and swallowing the turkey in his mouth.

"Shit, Grady, help me get this goddamn thing off the bed."

Grady raised an eyebrow but moved around the side of the truck. Lester reached in and maneuvered the lever to lower the bed to a forty-five degree angle. Grady carefully stepped up the newly formed ramp and gripped the motorcycle's handlebars. They were hot to the touch. Sure, it was summer and handles could definitely heat up in the sun, but it was the middle of the night when they'd brought it in but it felt like they had been baking in the afternoon sun for hours.

The whole thing had felt very odd indeed.

"Where'd this thing come from?" Grady asked.

Lester didn't look up as he retrieved a thick metal clipboard with a bunch of papers attached. "Fucking crazy, man. The guy riding this thing been on a killing spree up and down Route 539."

"*What?*" Grady hadn't heard anything about this, but it was surprising. The impound yard was civilian-owned and -operated so they rarely knew why a vehicle was brought in unless someone gave them the rundown. The attendants didn't just sit around listening to the police scanner all day. They mainly just read the paper or played games on their phones.

Lester still hadn't looked up as he hurriedly scribbled notes on the papers. He clearly wanted out of there as soon as possible. "Yeah, man. He killed six people in Lola's, then he took out the entire fucking police station. Must have slaughtered a dozen people."

"Holy shit," Grady muttered, eyeing the bike. "Who was he?"

"Fuck if I know," Lester replied, still not looking up. "And I'll tell you something else—" He handed the clipboard to Grady, who hesitantly accepted it. "—I don't wanna know."

"Did they get him?"

Lester made a twirling gesture with his finger, telling Grady to get on with it. He looked down and started signing.

"Yeah, the staties got there and put a bullet in his head. Guess I'm lucky that I just gotta dump off the bike. I'd hate to be in the meat wagon taking him to the morgue."

Grady handed the clipboard back to Lester without taking his eyes off the bike. He paused for a moment, but when he went to say something else, he heard the hydraulics fire in the tow truck. He turned to see that Lester was already back in the cab.

"What time you get off?" Lester asked him.

"7 a.m."

"Sucks to be you, dude," Lester said as he started the engine. "I'm peacing the fuck out of here. Later, man."

Lester backed the truck out a little too quickly, scraping the curb as he did. He shifted into drive and took off down the road, leaving a bewildered Grady alone with the motorcycle.

Christ, he was really spooked, Grady thought to himself as he moved over to the bike. *I mean sure, it's fucked up, but if the guy's dead—* He didn't finish his thought as another one entered his head. He stood next to the bike for a good five minutes, contemplating, before he awkwardly lifted one leg and straddled the seat, pausing for another moment before plopping himself down and gripping the handlebars again. They still felt hot, almost burning. He couldn't hold on for very long. He quickly released the bars and stepped off, stumbling in the process. Thankfully, he was able to maintain his balance and stay upright.

He had gone back to his booth and grabbed a pair of insulated gloves from the bottom drawer. He'd always wondered why they had been there and never really got a good answer, something about being for welders, but right now he was thankful that he had them. He donned the gloves and went back to the bike. Even with the added insulation, he was still hesitant to grab the handlebars again, but he did. He could still feel the heat through the gloves, but it was tolerable. He had moved the bike into the first available spot and walked as fast as he could back to the booth.

As dawn approached, Grady started to understand Lester's skittishness. The longer he sat there with the bike a hundred yards away, the more his anxiety grew. He couldn't pinpoint it, but it was there and got worse every hour. It was now almost 7 a.m. and Grady was practically jumping out of his chair, ready to go home.

Sometimes after a night shift he would stop at Lola's diner for breakfast. He especially loved when sweet little Courtney waited on him. She was an absolute doll. He knew there was no way she'd ever be into a tubby old parking lot attendant, but her warm smile and convivial tone always made him feel good, something that was typically in short supply in his life.

He felt his stomach twist into a knot. He'd been so bewildered by Lester's information that he hadn't stopped to wonder if Courtney was one of the people who got killed up at the diner. She had always been day shift, but he seemed to remember her telling him that she was picking up extra shifts whenever she could because she knew she'd be out for a few months after the baby was born. Her boyfriend didn't make all that much either, so they really needed the money. He really hoped that last night hadn't been one of those extra shifts.

He had no way of knowing. They didn't have any contact outside the diner and he had to imagine it would be closed down for a good long while. Maybe for good. He wasn't typically one for religion but he mouthed a silent prayer that she was okay. It actually made him feel guilty because many people had apparently been killed last night, but he was focused on his favorite waitress. He figured he should ask God to bless the families of the others too.

As he tried to figure out the logistics of how to pray, he heard a loud rattle come from the back of the lot, like something really shaking the fence.

What the hell?

He stood up and looked out the smudged windows of the booth. There was enough visibility but he didn't see anything other than rows of cars.

And the bike.

That damn motorcycle sat there. How could an inanimate object look like a rottweiler ready to pounce and rip your throat out? He didn't want to look at it any longer than he had to, so he went back to scanning the lot for signs of trouble.

Another loud rattle from the back.

He didn't want to leave the booth. He wasn't armed, a fact that he always took umbrage at. The owners expected the attendants to watch these vehicles owned by criminals without any kind of defense. Okay, maybe criminals was a bit of a stretch, since most of these were drunk drivers who were lucky enough that the cops had nabbed them before barreling headfirst into a tree or, worse, another vehicle. But still, there were some bad dudes who had their vehicles impounded here—like the mass-murdering motorcyclist.

Another loud rattle, followed by a thunk like something heavy hit the ground. Grady jumped. Something was definitely wrong. He continued to peer out the booth's windows as he fumbled for the phone on his desk. He picked it up and brought the receiver to his ear, expecting to hear the dial tone.

It was dead.

Grady pulled the phone away and looked at it as if there was going to be some physical defect that he could easily observe. There wasn't. The phone itself was fine, but the line was dead.

He reached into his pocket and pulled out his cell phone. He quickly dialed 911, but the call never started. He eyed the corner of the screen.

No service.

"Fuck!"

Working in a rural area, it wasn't uncommon to lose service from time to time, but did it really need to be the worst possible time? He didn't know what was causing the commotion in the back, but his sense of dread was thick and oppressive. As he pondered his next move, he saw a shadow move in the back of the lot.

Grady was a regular guy. He wasn't a cop. He was never in the military. The only fight he'd ever been in was in fifth grade and he lost decisively. He hit the button to open the front gate and dashed out of his booth. His car was toward the back where he'd seen the shadow, but maybe he could make it in time.

He couldn't. The shadow took shape as a man. He was too far away to make out the features, but there was no reason for anyone to be here at this hour, especially not for anyone to break in from the back. Grady had no interest in finding out, so he did the only thing he could think of.

He ran.

Grady moved as fast as his legs could take him, which wasn't very fast. He didn't make it far before his lungs started to burn and he tried desperately to suck in as much air as he could to replenish his overtaxed lungs.

As he heard the motorcycle roar to life behind him, he cursed the hoagie he had eaten a few hours ago. He cursed himself for never going to the gym or taking walks.

He kept his eyes forward as the motorcycle quickly closed ground and when he felt a large hand grip him by the back of the neck, he tried to pray again.

The hand inexplicably lifted his body off the ground. The wind smacked him in the face as he was carried alongside the speeding motorbike. He started to cry.

Right before his face smashed against the asphalt, he promised God that if he could somehow survive this, he would turn his life around.

His last thought as he died, was the knowledge that his prayer would go unanswered.

CHAPTER 13

Jeremy didn't realize he had fallen asleep until he was jolted awake. The last thing he remembered was going back inside and sitting in a waiting room chair while he waited for someone to get him to go see Ava. He must have passed out from exhaustion now that he felt safe for the first time since they'd pulled onto County Road 539 the day before. Without fear or adrenaline to keep him going, his body succumbed to exhaustion.

That is until he heard the unmistakable, seemingly impossible sound of the Rider's motorcycle approaching.

There was no denying that it was him. The sound that demon bike made was like no other. His stomach dropped as the rumble grew louder by the second, giving him precious little time to act. His head darted around looking for Bobby, but he couldn't see him. He must have still been outside finishing his joint. Jeremy had a quick inclination to run out and get him, but he had a more pressing concern. He opted to instead shout a warning, even though if Bobby was outside it was inconceivable that he was not aware of the danger barreling toward them.

"Bobby! He's here!"

CHAPTER 14

Ava awoke to screams.

She had been flirting with consciousness for what felt like hours at this point. The last thing she truly remembered was the massacre at the police station. She recalled walking outside before everything went black. Now she knew she was in a hospital bed and that a doctor had come to talk to her, telling her that some kind of procedure had went well. A blue curtain formed a horseshoe around the bed, blocking her off from the rest of the room. There were no windows so she couldn't tell if it was still nighttime. If she'd been more with it, she'd probably be able to surmise that she'd been here at least a day, but she was still fighting the effects of the anesthesia. She was confused and felt agitated in her mind, but was far too weak to put up any type of fight. While perplexed at her situation, she did not feel like she was in any type of physical danger.

Until now.

The terrified cries came from somewhere relatively distant, but they grew steadily louder as she started regaining control of her limbs.

She swallowed hard, her throat a desert, as she flexed her hands. A stabbing pinch emanated from the back of her left hand as she held it up to her sight line. She quickly identified the source of the discomfort as the intravenous tube stuck through her skin and held in place with white medical tape.

More muffled cries came from down the hall. She could only make out certain words or phrases, but her increasingly lucid brain told her that there was a panic in those halls.

"Jesus Christ!"

"Somebody call 911!"

"... a monster!"

Ava's eyes bulged as she understood that there was only one thing that could be causing that type of chaos.

The Rider. He was somehow still alive.

Her body's flight-or-fight response chose the latter as she sprang up in bed and ripped the IV out of her hand, a squirt of blood spattering the bed as she tossed it aside. She felt a draft on her back through the hospital gown, and the tile floor chilled the soles of her feet as she swung her legs over the side and off the bed.

She tried to stand, but her legs buckled and she crumpled to the floor, doing her best to brace herself as she fell.

She lay flat for a moment, wanting to stay there longer, but knowing that time was her enemy, she braced herself with her palms and pushed herself upward, turning into a seated position. She felt a searing heat radiate from her chest as she did.

A petrified shriek came from much closer than the previous ones. It rose and was quickly snuffed into a moist gurgle as God knows what happened to the source of the scream.

Ava placed her hands on the bedside table and tried to push herself up. Her slim frame may well have weighed three hundred pounds because her arms trembled from the effort, but failed to elevate her more than a few inches off the ground. Her sweat-slicked palms couldn't maintain contact with the surface and she slid off, slamming back into the ground with a hard slapping sound as she hit the tile again.

She wanted to scream in pain and frustration, but she knew any noise could be a death sentence at this point, so she clasped a hand over her mouth and used it to stifle a moan that she wished could have been a wail.

Ava quickly started crawling toward the curtain, knowing that even if she couldn't move, she also couldn't stay here.

She made it only a few inches before she heard a rapid clopping sound as a pair of legs adorned with blue scrubs and white sneakers came into her view. Mostly white that is, as they were speckled with red. The scrubs also had several dark spots that appeared wet, even through Ava's still hazy vision. She heard sobs in what sounded like a woman's voice as the person on the other side of the curtain hurried frantically away.

The soft footfalls of the sneakers were quickly drowned out by heavy, thudding steps, a sound that Ava had become too familiar with that evening. She froze and curled up, clasping her hands so tightly over her mouth that it would be impossible to make even the minutest sound.

Abruptly, the person tripped over their feet and fell to the floor right in front of Ava's curtain. She saw that it was indeed a woman and her forehead smacked the ground hard as she failed to brace herself for the impact.

The woman was a nurse, probably in her mid-forties, with a short bob with the roots showing through blonde dye. Ava thought that she wouldn't have an opportunity to dye it again, marveling at the odd thoughts that run through your head in a dangerous situation.

She saw that the woman was dazed as she slowly lifted her head off the ground, a gash bisecting her forehead almost straight down the middle. The woman looked at Ava through glazed over eyes and opened her mouth to say something.

Ava pleaded with the woman using her eyes, silently begging her not to give away her position. She had to realize there was nothing Ava could do to help her in her condition. She wished to God she could, but she couldn't.

The woman's mouth opened and shut, but no sound came out. Ava couldn't tell if that was because she had acquiesced to her wordless plea or if she had hit her head so hard she couldn't speak.

It didn't matter.

The now-familiar steel-toed boots straddled both sides of the helpless nurse as she rolled onto her back, gazing up at her attacker. Ava observed that the woman's entire outfit was wet and dark with blood, but it was unclear if it was hers or not.

The woman looked up wide-eyed and slowly opened her mouth, again not able to produce a sound.

Ava felt her eyes moisten as she kept her hands clasped over her mouth, mentally bracing herself for what she knew was about to happen.

The right boot rose up and disappeared above the curtain, remaining out of view for a moment before it came back down hard on the woman's head. It exploded, not unlike the poor waitress's a few hours earlier, only this time it wasn't from a shotgun blast, it was from the sheer force of this animal's foot. Chunks of skull and brain escaped from around the foot which had come down so hard that Ava was shocked it hadn't shattered the tile the same way it had her skull.

She screamed internally, but still managed to not make a sound. Knowing that she was only a moment away from the same fate or worse (Was there worse? Again, those weird thoughts borne of peril) she did the only thing she could think of.

With every modicum of strength in her body, Ava rolled under the bed and, hopefully, out of sight.

When she settled in her hiding place, she adjusted herself back onto her stomach and peered out from under the bed and beyond the curtain to see that the position of the killer and his victim had not changed – his right boot was still embedded in what was left of her head.

Her stomach churned. She felt like she might vomit, but her stomach was empty so she gave little more than a gag and a dry heave.

She mouthed a silent prayer. She hadn't always been the most religious, but if there were ever a time to ask for help from a higher power, this was it.

The foot rose out of the ruined cranium, strands of brain matter hanging from it as if it had just stepped in gooey, fresh gum. Ava realized her prayer had gone unanswered when the foot came back down and slowly turned toward the still closed curtain.

"No, no, no, no, no," Ava said in her head over and over again, even though she knew it wouldn't prevent what would come next.

The killer ripped the curtain down as the fabric and the rod fell next to the dead nurse with a clank. The black pants were unmistakable. How was this possible? How was he alive? He had taken a bullet straight to the head.

The feet stepped over the downed barrier and moved to the side of the bed. Ava remained on her stomach, not wanting to turn on her side to track his path. Maybe if she didn't move, he'd just look around and head back out.

He didn't.

Ava finally screamed as a hand reached under the bed and, in one deft movement, gripped the rails and tossed it over as if it were a card table, exposing the terrified woman underneath.

As if there were any doubt, Ava saw that it was indeed the Rider; only now he was not wearing his helmet or face cover and his mangled visage was on full display. There was flesh on his face, but it was torn and tattered, hanging off the bones of his skull, which was visible in more than a few spots. What skin was left was rotten and gray, a fetid stench assaulting Ava's nostrils.

Speaking of nostrils, that's all he had, with no remnant of a nose remaining. His eyes, which Ava had felt on her several times that day, even though obscured, were a milky white, both in the iris and the pupil but, despite the fact that they looked dead, there was life in them, an amalgamation of rage, pain and desire wrapped in a piercing package.

"Why are you doing this to me?" Ava cried. "Why?"

The Rider cocked his head but remained ever silent. Ava could do nothing but lie there and sob. As the seconds bore on, she became aware that the killing blow had not yet come.

With seemingly no options left, Ava twisted her fear into defiance, determined that if she was going to die today, she would go out on her feet, at least figuratively.

"Fuck you!" she screamed, her throat stinging through the effort.

The Rider tilted his head back into an upright position, but still did not do anything other than observe.

"What the fuck are you waiting for, asshole?"

Whatever it was, she didn't find out as a blast of foamy white smoke engulfed her stalker, the shock knocking him back. She turned to see Bobby brandishing a fire extinguisher, spraying him full blast.

While Bobby kept him occupied, a shape emerged around his right side and barreled toward the shape of the Rider. It was another man. He lowered his shoulder and slammed into him, knocking him back. The impact was enough to move him to where he tripped over the downed curtain, sending him crashing against a metal tray with a plastic purple cup and a pack of unopened saltine crackers, likely there to get something into Ava's stomach to stifle the after-effects of the anesthesia. The tray clattered to the ground, splashing the water and crushing the crackers.

Ava tried to make sense of what was happening as a pair of strong, familiar hands gripped under her armpits and lifted her into a standing position. As the man wrapped one of her arms around the back of the neck, she saw that it was Jeremy. She hadn't thought it possible to be even happier to see him than she usually was.

"I'm out!" Bobby's voice penetrated the smoke. "Let's get the fuck out of here."

Jeremy didn't respond. He simply kept one hand on Ava's wrist around his neck and wrapped the other around her waist. Although she did her best to move, he carried her more than anything.

Ava inadvertently caught a mouthful of the smoke from the extinguisher and coughed loudly as they made their way through the cloud. When it cleared, she saw Bobby toss the red extinguisher in the Rider's direction.

It hit something, but it was impossible to tell if it was him or not.

Bobby grabbed Ava's other arm and draped it around his own neck, allowing the trio to pick up speed to make their escape. They made their way down the hall to a pair of heavy wooden double doors, the only thing standing between themselves and freedom. Two windows would have provided a view to the waiting room if they weren't completely soaked in blood. Bobby turned and thrust his shoulder into the door, cursing as it didn't budge.

"Fuck!"

Jeremy looked around for a switch but didn't see it. There was only a rectangular black device, about the size of a deck of cards on the wall. A pin-sized red light indicated that it was a sensor, typically requiring a key card.

"Shit! We need a card!" Jeremy said, stating the obvious.

He scanned the room, looking for a solution or an alternate escape route. Ava weakly chimed in.

"Behind... the desk? Check behind the desk!"

Jeremy reacted quickly, making sure that Bobby could hold Ava up steady before he ran over to the large circular desk in the center of the room. He hopped over to the other side and saw a man in dark-blue scrubs sprawled out on the ground, his throat slit from ear to ear. It was a testament to the horror of the night that he no longer flinched at the sight of a dead body.

"Jeremy! Hurry!" Ava's voice cried in panic.

He instinctively looked up to see the Rider emerge from around the corner. He stopped and looked at the trio with his dead eyes, transfixing them momentarily before he started moving around the desk.

"Fuck!" Jeremy exclaimed as he reached down and snatched the name tag clipped to the corpse's bloodstained pocket.

It detached easily and he quickly moved to jump back over the desk, only this time his foot got caught and he dropped hard on the other side, wailing as he came down hard on his injured shoulder.

"Jeremy!" Ava shouted. "Get up!"

The Rider was only a scant few feet away. Jeremy tossed the badge to Bobby, who managed to catch it clean.

"Get her out of here!" he shouted to them.

"No! What are you doing?" Ava screamed.

"Now!"

Bobby swiped the card against the reader and the doors slowly opened. He didn't wait from them to fully open. Instead he twisted himself and Ava to the side and squeezed through as soon as the opening was wide enough.

"We can't leave him!" Ava protested as she saw the Rider descend on her husband. She pummeled her fists against Bobby, but not hard enough to make an impact in her weakened condition. She saw the Rider grab Jeremy's shirt by the collar and lift him to his feet as Bobby dragged her toward the exit while the doors closed behind him.

"No! Jeremy!"

CHAPTER 15

Ava pleaded with Bobby as they exited the hospital, the late-afternoon sun assaulting her eyes, confirming that she had been in the hospital for at least half a day at this point. "Please! We have to go back."

Bobby shook his head. "Darling, we can't go back. He'll fucking slaughter us."

"But Jeremy..."

"He's gone. I'm sorry."

Ava felt her soul constrict at the thought. They'd just got married. She was the one who was supposed to die young, not him. How was any of this fair? All they wanted to do was be together, to live and to love and this motherfucker had stolen that from them.

"We have to fucking kill him," Ava said through gritted teeth.

Bobby carried her to the closest car, a jet-black BMW, probably belonging to one of the doctors. They all seemed to love their Beemers.

"Brace yourself, Ava," he said as he guided her hands to the trunk, giving her the briefest of seconds to steady herself. She felt like she would collapse and her hands shook as she held on, but she managed to stay on her feet.

Bobby bent his right arm and placed his left hand on his right fist, using it to thrust his right elbow into the passenger side window, shattering it. He hit the unlock button and yanked the door open, grabbing Ava and ushering her inside as fast as he could before running around to the opposite side and getting in himself.

Ava turned and looked out the back window, desperately hoping that somehow Jeremy was okay. That he would emerge from the hospital and jump in the car with them.

But he didn't.

Bobby had yanked a panel open under the steering wheel and had pulled some wires out. He grabbed one of the bigger shards of glass from the broken window and used it to cut one of the wires in half, before stripping it to expose the copper underneath. He flicked them together, causing a spark, but nothing else. He repeated the process, two, three, four more times.

"C'mon, you fucking cunt!" he shouted.

Ava was becoming less hopeful that it would be Jeremy who walked out and more concerned that it would be the Rider. Without a working vehicle, they were sitting ducks.

More flicking, more cursing.

"Should we try another car?" Ava asked.

"Time ain't exactly on our side, kid."

He flicked the wires together again and this time the engine roared to life. He held the two copper ends together and twisted them so they stayed connected.

"Thank Christ!" he exclaimed through a relieved exhalation.

He tossed the car into gear and backed out of the spot. As he did, Ava noticed a man emerge from the hospital. Her heart leaped into her throat.

"Jeremy!" she shouted. "It's Jeremy! Don't go yet!"

Bobby shifted into drive, but kept his foot on the brake, ready to accelerate at a moment's notice.

Ava looked Jeremy over as he hobbled toward them. His leg was bloody and he was favoring his arm, but he was moving as fast as he could, a sign that Ava hoped meant he wasn't seriously injured. She leaned out of the broken window, mindful not to cut herself on the shards of glass remaining in the door.

"Jeremy! Baby! Over here!"

His eyes betrayed desperation as he tried to pick up his pace even more. Ava felt terror in the pit of her stomach as she realized the Rider was on his heels.

"Faster!" she screamed at him. "He's coming! Please hurry!"

Jeremy tried his hardest. His face was the visage of a man who wanted to live, a man who was not ready to leave the world, not ready to leave his wife and unborn child. He fought with every fiber of his being. He tried his best, but it wasn't good enough.

He fell.

Ava screamed at the top of her lungs as she watched him lose his balance and hit the blacktop.

The Rider, much like in the hospital, straddled him and grabbed his collar, yanking him upward. The difference was that now he was brandishing his machete. It wasn't clear when he had retrieved it. It had likely been embedded in some poor soul who had met their end during the assault as it was caked in blood, some fresh, some practically part of the steel at this point. It didn't matter. He had it and there was no doubt what he was going to do with it.

"Please!" Ava begged, knowing it wouldn't do any good. "Please let him go."

The last words choked off in her throat, becoming a whisper. She knew whatever this thing was, it was not human. It did not possess emotion and it was not prone to reason. She sobbed as she readied to watch her world well and truly fall apart.

She saw a single tear fall down Jeremy's cheek as he mouthed the words, "I love you."

"*No!*" she shrieked louder than ever as she saw Jeremy's shirt stretch and then tear at the stomach as the blade protruded through him, pouring blood down the front of his pants and pooling at his knees. The Rider twisted the blade and pulled it back out, opening the wound wider, causing his entrails to spill out in front of him as the weapon made its exit.

"I'm sorry," Bobby said as he stomped his foot down on the accelerator. The tires screeched as the car peeled out of the parking lot.

Ava watched her husband slump dead to the ground. Even though she could live a thousand lifetimes and never see anything more devastating, she didn't take her eyes off of him until the car rounded a corner and she lost sight of him.

CHAPTER 16

Ava opened her eyes and immediately squinted as sunlight unexpectedly washed over her. She brought a cupped hand up to her forehead as she blinked a few times, trying to clear up her vision. It was hot. Very hot. The heat of an afternoon in mid-August. She felt the sweat on her brow as her hand made contact.

She was lying down on a piece of cloth on an uneven surface, realizing it was a towel resting on sand. The sound of waves gently crashing into the shore and receding, along with the occasional squawk of a seagull told her she was back on the beach. She had no idea how she had gotten back. Her instinct was to sit up, but she opted to lie there for a few moments. The heat was intense but it felt good on her tired body. She closed her eyes and folded her hands over her stomach, which was bare, as she was wearing her bikini. She felt a lump in her throat at the realization. How did she get here? She felt a slight flutter in her stomach. Unlike anything she'd ever felt before. It was just the tiniest of movements, but it was different. She wasn't scared though. It somehow comforted her.

"You feel him?" a voice asked.

Ava gasped. She recognized it and bolted upward, turning her head.

She was indeed on the beach in Atlantic City, except it was completely empty. Not a soul on the shore or the boardwalk.

Except for Jeremy. He sat on the towel next to her, beaming that smile of his as a few strands of his long hair fell loose and hung over his eyes. He was wearing the clothes he had put on that morning before they'd checked out.

"Jeremy?" she asked in a confused, tear-choked voice.

"Hi," he said.

Tears dripped down her cheeks as relief washed over her. It was all a nightmare. Jeremy was here and he was okay. She threw her arms around him and squeezed him tighter than she ever had, closing her eyes and taking in the feel of his body, the scent of his cologne. Everything was just the way she knew it. He reciprocated by putting his own arms around her, albeit gentler. His embrace was clearly intended as a gesture of comfort. Ava held him desperately as if he would slip away forever if she let go.

"You were having a bad dream, baby."

Ava gasped out a sob she hadn't noticed she'd been holding in. "It was... it was horrible."

"I know."

"I thought I lost you."

"I'm sorry."

"It's okay. You're here. Everything is okay now."

"I wish I could tell you it was."

Ava held on, but opened her eyes. "What?"

Jeremy gently unwrapped his arms from around her and tenderly clasped his hand on each arm, gently guiding her back. As he did, she noticed that she was no longer wearing a bikini, but a dirty, blood-spattered hospital gown. Something was very wrong.

"What... no... no."

Jeremy lifted her chin so he could look her in the eyes. "You have to listen to me, Ava."

"No..."

"There isn't much time."

She didn't want to look down, but she did. She saw the wound in his stomach. The blood. The guts. A puddle of viscera staining the beach towel. She wanted to scream but couldn't.

"Look at me, baby."

She looked back up and Jeremy's blue eyes were dead and gray. Not unlike the Rider's.

"No, Jeremy, no," she repeated.

He didn't try to comfort her. His voice carried a new urgency.

"You don't have much time. I know you're sad. I know you're scared. But you have to listen to me."

"I don't understand..."

"He's not going to stop. You know that."

Ava closed her eyes and nodded.

"What happened to me is not your fault. None of this is your fault."

"What am I going to do without you?"

"You're going to go on. You're going to live. Most importantly, you're going to fight."

"Fight?" she asked, a hint of unintentional anger in the question. "How am I supposed to fight that thing?"

"I don't know. I wish I did. I just know that you can't give up."

Now the anger emerged full force. "Why? Why the fuck do I have to fight? You're dead. What's left for me? A couple more years with a bad fucking heart? It was already broken. How am I supposed to handle this?"

She unleashed a primal scream at the top of her lungs, the wind carrying it out over the crashing waves of the Atlantic Ocean, the sky beginning to darken as the tide rolled in.

Jeremy let her have the release.

When she was done, she looked at him through bloodshot, apologetic eyes. "I'm scared, Jeremy. I need you."

"I'm sorry. I can't be there for you. Till death do us part, right?"

"It wasn't supposed to be like this."

"I know, but you have to be strong." Ava started to say something else, but Jeremy cut her off by placing his hand on her stomach. She felt that flutter again as he continued. "You have to be strong for him."

Ava didn't understand at first. She looked down and put her hand over Jeremy's and felt another movement. It was unmistakable. It was a kick. She looked back at him. He was himself again. The blood was gone. His eyes were their normal blue.

"I know you said you didn't want this, but I know you did. You have to fight and you have to live for our baby. Because he will be the only thing left of me."

"He?" Ava asked.

Jeremy smiled. "I love you, Ava."

He kissed her and got up.

She grabbed his arm to stop. "Don't go."

He gave her a sympathetic look. "You know I have to."

"Why?" she pleaded, not trying to mask the desperation in her voice.

"Fight for him, Ava. He's your reason now."

Jeremy gently but firmly pulled his arm away and started to walk down the beach. Ava looked back down at her stomach and pressed her hand firmly, perplexed by what just happened. Although she had maintained for years that she couldn't have kids, she knew she wanted this more than anything. She also knew that Jeremy was right. She had to fight, not just for her, but for their child. She just didn't know how.

"Jeremy!" she called as she looked back up.

He was gone.

CHAPTER 17

Ava gasped as she shot forward in the passenger seat of the stolen BMW. She instinctively managed to get her hands up to block her head from slamming against the dashboard since she was not wearing a seatbelt.

"Jeremy!" she uttered breathlessly.

Bobby swerved from the shock of Ava jumping forward, but the road was empty save for them, so he was able to adjust quickly and without incident.

"Jesus Christ! You scared the shit out of me."

Ava observed him with bloodshot eyes, the combination of physical trauma, grief and anesthesia taking a clear toll on the young woman. She didn't say anything. Didn't know what to say. Jeremy was dead and they were far from safe. The situation seemed hopeless.

She turned and looked out the front window. She must have been out for a while, because dusk was quickly transitioning to night. Bobby flicked the headlights on as Ava could tell it was getting difficult to see the road ahead.

"Where are we going?" she asked weakly.

"I got an idea."

"What idea?"

Bobby leaned forward and peered ahead like he was looking for something. "I'll explain when we get there."

"Where?"

"Just trust me, okay?"

Trusting a stranger she'd only known for a day would have normally been a big ask, but these were not normal circumstances. Not to mention that this old outlaw had saved her more than once in the past twenty-four hours. There was no apparent safe haven. A diner. A police station. A hospital. All their occupants massacred because this thing—and it was not human, Ava was convinced of that now—wanted her for some unknown purpose. The only thing she figured they could do was to keep moving. To try to stay ahead of it. That was their only chance, but realistically how long could they keep this up? Bobby was a broken-down old biker who may be just as much of a target as she was—after all he was the one who killed Caleb the first time—and she was limited by her illness. She started to cry because she could not see a way that it wouldn't eventually catch him.

"It'll be okay," Bobby said unconvincingly.

Ava thought about asking him to find somewhere where there was a phone so she could call her parents. They surely knew something was wrong at this point and must be out of their minds with worry. She put that thought out of her head though. She couldn't contact them. It would almost certainly put them in danger. She'd already lost Jeremy; she didn't know what she'd do if she lost them too.

While she contemplated her situation, Bobby abruptly turned off the road and into the woods, the car jostling them about as they transitioned from pavement to a dirt road.

"What are you doing?"

"There may be only one thing that can stop him."

"You just took us onto a dirt road into the woods; I appreciate everything you've done for us, but I need some answers right now, Bobby.

"We have to get Vicki."

"*What?*"

"This is all about you and it ain't no coincidence that you look exactly like Caleb's girl. There has to be something we missed when we buried her and the only way we're going to find out what is to dig her up."

"*Dig her up?* Is that really going to help us kill this thing?"

"Dunno, but I'm fresh out of ideas and right now you and me are the only two living souls who know who he is and what happened all them years ago."

Ava felt her insides twist in a knot. The last thing she wanted to do was dig up a twenty-year-old corpse just on the off chance that it might hold the key to stopping that monster. But Bobby was right. They were one hundred percent out of options, so it was time for a hail Mary.

"You said this happened twenty years ago? How do you even know where she'll be?"

"Don't you worry. I know."

As they made their way deeper into the pines, Ava was surprised at just how far in the road took them. The woods were so much deeper than she expected. After what felt like an hour, but in reality was more like five minutes, the road came to an end and Bobby stopped the car, killing the engine. The headlights went away, leaving only darkness.

"How far is it?" Ava asked.

"About a mile."

"A *mile*?"

Ava immediately contemplated all the ways that seemed like a bad idea. She had gotten winded hiking through the woods yesterday when she was in significantly better physical condition and now she was going to have to do it again after her heart had stopped and she'd had surgery the night before. How could she make the walk now? Beyond that, she couldn't see two feet in front of her.

"How are you going to find the way with no light?"

Bobby huffed. He clearly hadn't considered that part of it. He thought about it for a moment and then searched below the steering wheel until he found the right button. He pressed it and something clicked behind them. He opened his door.

"Wait here."

Ava watched as he made his way behind the car to the open trunk. She heard him rooting around inside, but couldn't make out what he was doing. It became clear, in more ways than one, a few moments later when a warm yellow light illuminated the woods. Luckily for them there was a heavy-duty flashlight in the trunk.

"C'mon Ava. Let's get moving."

They made their way through the woods mostly in silence, save for the cracking of twigs and leaves under their feet. Ava did her best to maneuver, but the surgical socks she wore—a fluffy pair with grippers on the bottom, were not a good substitute for hiking boots and she felt a stabbing ache in her soles as they moved along.

For his part, Bobby kept a slow but steady pace, holding out the flare in front of them. It provided pretty decent light, but Ava also couldn't help but feel nervous at just how bright it was. If that thing was behind them, they wouldn't be hard to spot. Bobby held her hand to make sure she kept pace. His hands were dirty, sweaty and rough, but Ava took in what little comfort she should. At least she wasn't alone. Without him pushing her forward she could easily see herself just dropping on the spot and letting her grief overtake her.

"Oh, Jeremy. How am I going to do this without you?" she thought to herself as she placed her free hand gently over her stomach.

"Here," Bobby said, his voice stamping out her thoughts.

"Huh?" Ava asked dreamily as she squinted to see through the light.

It was a shack.

"What is this?" she asked.

Bobby turned to face her. "I need you to wait here."

"What? Are you insane?"

Bobby frowned and gestured his open palm toward her feet, specifically the socks which had become tattered, torn and caked with mud.

"I still got a ways to go to get to the site and the terrain is only getting rougher. I need you to take shelter in here."

"In here?" she asked with disbelief. "Isn't this the shack where it happened?"

"Yeah, it is," Bobby replied. "But its got four walls and a roof... kind of."

Ava looked up and saw that a tree branch had fallen and partially collapsed one side of the structure.

"You can duck down and stay out of sight. Out here you're exposed."

"What if it finds me?"

"Then you'll be grateful for the rest when you have to run."

Ava must have looked like a deer in headlights.

"Listen," Bobby continued, "the quicker I get out there, the quicker I get back and we can end this shit."

"And if we can't?"

"Then we keep running. Or die."

Bobby ushered her inside. There was no floor to speak of, only dirt with some sparse tufts of grass and weeds scattered about. A wooden table sat off to one corner. It was partially eaten by termites and looked like it would collapse if she put so much as a piece of paper on top of it. Underneath were the remains of a single chair which had been reduced to little more than scraps. A lot of the wood was darkly discolored. Ava didn't want to think about it, but it was clearly blood that had soaked in.

The place just felt wrong. It was late August and still hot even at this late hour, but Ava felt a chill run through her body as she stood on this site of so much pain and bloodshed. She thought of her other in the mirror. Vicki. A girl who had looked so much like her it spurred a rampage of death and destruction she would have never thought possible. It was like she was some dime-store Helen of Troy. The face that launched a monster on a motorcycle. Jesus Christ, she doubted anyone could write something that absurd if they tried.

On the other side was a cot. There were no sheets or pillows, just a filthy old mattress with a myriad of ugly dark stains. She tried not to think too hard about what they actually were. A few springs popped up through the mattress, somehow making sitting on it even less appealing, an idea she didn't think possible.

After surveying both sides, she looked the one place she didn't want to. Dead in the center of the room was a wooden post with a large spike embedded near the top. She felt dizzy as she looked at it and her vision blurred. She blinked hard to try to clear it. When she opened her eyes, she wished she hadn't.

She saw Vicki, clear as day, gagged and bound, with the ropes tying her hands looped around the spike, keeping her arms in a raised position. She was naked, her body familiar to Ava; like her face, it was indiscernible from her own. She also had a tattoo on her ribcage, just like her, although Ava could not make out what it said due to the blood. It trickled from numerous deep cuts that covered her body. The cuts formed shapes and symbols. She had no idea what they meant but they looked like something out of *The Lord of the Rings*. Whatever they were, they had been deliberately and slowly etched into her skin and she was sobbing softly through her gag, no doubt in agonizing pain.

It had to be a vision. It couldn't be real. Still, Ava's eyes met hers and she knew that Vicki could see her too. Somehow they were looking at each other across time. Her eyes pleaded for help, but Ava didn't know how she could. She looked over to Bobby, wanting to ask if he was seeing it too, but he was off in the corner, looking through a large cabinet that she had not noticed when they entered, likely because it was obscured by the door. She turned back and Vicki was gone again.

"Okay," Bobby said, getting her attention.

She turned back from the post and focused on her companion. He was holding a shovel. She had wondered if he intended to dig her up with his bare hands, but he must have known that there was a shovel here. They must have left it after they buried Caleb and Vicki all those years ago.

"How long will you be?" she asked.

"If I find the spot right away, hopefully not more than an hour."

"An hour?"

"Kid, I ain't in my twenties no more. I don't know how long it's going to take to dig up a damn body and carry it back here!"

Ava sighed. She knew he was right. "Okay. Just... hurry."

"I'll do my best."

He gave her shoulder a squeeze, trying to reassure her. It didn't have the intended effect.

"Stay low," he said before exiting the cabin.

Ava hadn't realized she'd fallen back asleep, but as exhausted as her body was, it wasn't a surprise. She chose to sit on the mattress, her back against the wall of the shack. She'd been covered in blood, gore and dirt the better part of the two days now so a dirty mattress wasn't exactly beyond the pale at this point. She woke up when she heard footsteps approaching. They were heavy, but not the ponderous thuds of the Rider's footfalls. It had to be Bobby.

Sure enough, the door opened and Bobby hurried inside, slamming the door behind him as he tossed the shovel on the ground. He grabbed the cabinet and unceremoniously dumped it on its side, a few assorted tools like hedge clippers and rakes tumbling out as it hit the ground. He grasped it on either side and dragged it over in front of the door, barricading it.

"What's going on?" Ava said noticing he hadn't been carrying anything other than the shovel. "Did you find her?"

"There ain't much time now," he said as he looked out the window.

"Did you hear him?" Ava said jumping off the cot. "Is he here?"

"Not yet," Bobby said.

"So where's Vicki?"

Ava barely got the question out before Bobby's meat hook of a fist hit her right between the eyes.

She saw stars.

Then darkness.

CHAPTER 18

Ava's eyes opened. How many times that she had lost consciousness since this nightmare began? If she somehow made it out alive, she would likely contemplate just how much of a toll these events had taken on her body and wonder just how much her heart could ultimately withstand. Frankly, it was a miracle that she had survived to this point. But, given her current situation, it was hard to see that lasting much longer.

The first thing she noticed was the pain directly below her forehead, no doubt the result of Bobby's sucker punch. She also felt soreness in her armpits and wrists. The pain gave way to fear when she realized that her wrists were tied and the rope was slung over the spike, holding her arm upright, just like Vicki in her vision. She looked down and saw that she was still wearing her hospital gown. Thank God. At least she didn't have to suffer the indignity of being naked on top of everything else.

She observed the shack through watery eyes. Her nose throbbed and her lips felt wet. She instinctively ran her tongue over them and tasted a coppery liquid. Blood. She couldn't smell it, though. Her nose must be broken. That motherfucker. What was he doing? Given the minuscule size of the structure, it didn't take long to locate Bobby over in the corner. He was hunched over the downed cabinet rummaging around. He looked different now. He was wearing his cut, Hell's Horde M.C. logo big and bold, stretched across his back.

"What the fuck are you doing?" Ava screamed.

Bobby jumped, not having realized that his captive had regained consciousness.

"Christ, girl. You scared the shit outta me."

Ava shot daggers at him with her eyes, a gesture not lost on the old biker. He met her eyes with sympathy, but as the old saying goes, you'll find that in the dictionary between shit and syphilis.

"Why?" she asked. Quieter this time.

"It ain't personal, kid. Like I said, we gotta end this shit."

Ava was beyond confused. "What about Vicki?"

"Vicki's a pile of bones in a hole in the woods. She ain't helping us."

"Then why did you go out there?"

Bobby reached inside the vest and produced a folded, yellowed piece of paper. It looked like a page torn from a book.

"For this," Bobby said as he unfolded the paper and looked it over. "This is the key."

"What is that?"

"When we busted in on Caleb and Vicki that night, he was doing some sort of ritual. That explains them symbols he cut into her."

He moved in and held up the page for Ava to see. The paper looked very old, not just evident by the yellowing, but the fraying of the pages around the edges. It looked like it could crumble in his hands. Ava recalled a field trip she took in eighth grade to Washington DC. One of the stops on the trip was the National Archives where she observed the original Declaration of Independence. The page reminded her of that, although somehow it looked even older than that document that was more than two hundred years old itself. It looked... ancient.

"He had this on him. It was the instructions. We buried it with him. Didn't seem right to leave it around for anyone else to see."

"Why didn't you just burn it, you fucking moron?"

Bobby just shrugged. "We didn't know what this was. It seemed damn important. We figured we may need it some day. And look. Here we are."

The text was illegible. It wasn't in any language she knew, just a series of odd and ominous-looking symbols. The only thing that was discernible was the outline of a human figure. Inside the lines were more strange symbols, all over the figure's legs, arms and torso. What did this all mean?

"How do you know what this gibberish says? You look like you have trouble with the English alphabet. How you going to figure this shit out?" Ava said, unable to stop herself from being defiant.

Bobby just laughed. "You got spirit, girl. I like you. I wish this could have gone down different."

"It can," Ava replied. "Just let me go."

Bobby flipped the page in his hand and showed her the back. There were handwritten notes on the back. They were in plain English and outlined the instructions from the carving of the symbols to the incantation to be chanted. The words were mostly unfamiliar, but someone could probably sound them out phonetically without much trouble. It was called the "Rite of Atonement." From what she could see it was a ceremony undertaken as penance for wronging one's god. Worshippers were granted a favor or favors in return for services. If those services were not performed, a sacrifice was required.

"I can't. I'm sorry."

Ava spit in his face. Her saliva was mixed with blood, confirming that her nose was bleeding. Bobby closed his eyes and calmly wiped the mess off his face with his forearm.

"Fuck you!"

Bobby took a deep, resigned breath. "I get it, kid. None of this shit is fair. I didn't plan this. I really tried to help you two. That was real. But after the police station, then the hospital, I realized that he isn't going to stop coming for you."

"Why?" she bellowed. "What the fuck did I do to deserve any of this?"

"Caleb pissed off his boss. I don't know who this Bill guy was, but he wasn't just some gun runner or drug dealer. He was something that I don't get. Somehow he was able to give Caleb everything he ever wanted overnight. Anyone who can do that has power. Power that no man can explain. When a man with that power gives you something, it comes with a price. And if you can't pay it, you'll have hell to pay instead. He sold his goddamn soul to get that girl and when he couldn't pay the vig, Bill took the girl back. Only he needed to add another layer to Caleb's penance. He had to be the one to do the deed."

Ava couldn't believe what she was hearing. Who was this Bill guy? The fucking devil? But even if she looked just like her, she wasn't Vicki. What good would killing her do?

"So you're going to finish what Caleb started with me instead of Vicki? How do you know that would even work?"

Bobby sighed. "I don't."

"Then why?" she yelled.

"Because we're out of fucking options!" he screamed back. "Micah, Eddie and me fucked up. We thought we were doing the right thing, but all we did is create something worse. If we just let him finish that fucked-up sacrifice, none of this shit would have happened. You'd be on your way home and your husband and all them other people would still be alive."

"So you're a fucking humanitarian now?" Ava asked, her defiance returning. "You give a shit about all those poor people? You give a shit about Jeremy?"

His name choked in her throat as the mention of it brought intense grief to the forefront.

"No. I'm just an old outlaw who's trying to live another day. It ain't some poetic bullshit. But, my selfishness will probably save some lives. So that'll have to be enough."

Ava struggled against her restraints, trying to kick him, but he easily stepped back out of her line of attack.

"What good is it going to do for you to finish the ritual? You're not the one that wronged Bill."

Bobby didn't answer. He went back over to the cabinet and produced a rusted three-pronged hand rake. The middle prong was bent forward, not aligned with the others.

"This'll have to do. I really am sorry, Ava."

He moved toward her as she thrashed about. He grabbed her by the neck and squeezed, his large hands cutting off her scream in her windpipe.

"Stay still," he said. "You're only going to make this worse."

She tried to talk, but couldn't. She thrashed around a bit more until fatigue overtook her. Once she settled, Bobby removed his hand and she felt the air rush back into her lungs as she coughed violently, tasting the blood once again.

"It's not going to work."

"It will," Bobby said, looking over the diagram on the page.

"Why will it work for you?"

Her question was cut off by a cry of pain as Bobby made the first cut just below her bicep. A curved line that was not deep, but still drew a decent amount of blood.

"Because I'm not the one who's going to finish it."

CHAPTER 19

The Rider saw the flare on the asphalt on the side of the road. It was by same path that he had chased down that fat old man and took his head. The red cloud was a contrast against the black night sky. He pulled his bike up to the flare and turned his gaze toward the woods. Another light, bright and yellowish as if from a powerful flashlight, was barely visible in the distance. It was a beacon that he knew was meant for him. She was close. Why would they give away their position? Had they become resigned to their fate? It didn't matter. He would continue his pursuit until the end. They couldn't stop him.

He twisted the handlebars of the motorcycle and started his ride down the path. He felt an eerie sense of calm for the first time. Since his re-awakening, so much of what he had done was driven by rage and hatred, his anger spurring him onward. But now he felt content that an end was approaching. She would finally be sacrificed and his suffering would come to an end. So close.

The flashlight illuminated the path that extended deeper into the forest. The Rider stopped his bike and dismounted, picking up the beaming cylinder and examining it. He lifted it and pointed the beam off into the distance. He didn't need any more markers to know where they guided him. He knew where the shack was and could find it even in total darkness.

He stepped forward, his heavy boot snapping a branch in his way.

Nothing would stop him now.

CHAPTER 20

Ava cried as the rusty prong cut her again, this time just below her left shoulder blade. It stung and burned as the metal ripped into her flesh.

"You fucker!" she screamed at Bobby as he worked.

He didn't reply. Surely he knew there was no more to say. To him, this was the only option and she couldn't convince him otherwise.

She still wore the tattered hospital gown, Bobby cutting in the already-exposed areas as if somehow he was trying to preserve her dignity as long as he could, although that was the least of her concerns right now.

"Stop! Please!" she cried, her voice hoarse and raw.

The pain seared her. Her body was a symphony of agony conducted by an orchestra of cuts, scrapes and bruises. Add that to the fact that a doctor burned scar tissue from the surface of her heart the night before and needless to say, Ava had never experienced hurt like this.

"Sit still!" Bobby demanded. "You're only making this worse."

"Fuck you!" Ava cried. A familiar refrain by now, but really all she had.

Bobby paused and inspected the derelict paper in his hands, looking perplexed as he muttered to himself.

"Is that a square or a rectangle?"

"Guess you failed geometry, you fucking moron."

Ava found herself surprised at just how brazen she was given her predicament. But fuck it. Better to go out on her feet then her knees.

Bobby slapped her in the mouth. Hard. That copper taste again.

"I'm trying not to make this any harder than it has to be, but I'm telling you right now to shut the fuck up."

Ava spit more blood out of her mouth, at his feet this time. She wanted to resist, but she was more than aware that she had limited recourse at the moment.

"So you think that thing's just going to show up here and just let you go when it sees you have me tied up?"

"All he seems to want is you. What would he want me for then?"

"You fucking shot Caleb dead. You think it doesn't remember?"

Bobby's face went white. Had he really not considered that little factoid? He shook it off. "Don't matter," he said, turning his attention back to the piece of paper. "I'll just buy some time and get the fuck out of Dodge."

"How do you think you're going to do that?"

Bobby reached under his vest down the back of his jeans and came back with a handgun. It looked like the ones the police officers where using.

"Took this off of one of the dead cops while everyone was distracted. Figured it'd come in handy. He comes at me, I'll plug him again. By the time he gets back up, I'll be gone and he can finish up with you."

Ava let out a scream through gritted teeth and tried to lunge forward. The rope held her in place, but something felt different. She felt the post give, just a little.

Bobby cracked her again, knocking her silly as she slumped backward.

"Just. Stop," he said. "This will all be over soon."

A twig snapped outside, the sound bringing Ava back to her senses. She looked up and tried to tilt her head to see out the window, but there was nothing but darkness.

"Caleb?" Bobby called toward the door. "That you?"

Ava heard more rustling outside, but it was still just the two of them as far as she could tell.

"Caleb!" Bobby shouted again. "I got her. She's ready for you!"

Still no response.

"Yeah, Caleb!" Ava chimed in. "Listen to the guy who shot you! You really think you can trust him?"

Bobby pulled out the pistol again and stomped over to Ava, pressing the barrel hard underneath her chin. The metal felt cold against her roughed-up skin.

"Shut your fucking mouth."

As he pressed against her, she felt the post move again. This was her chance. She knew what she had to do.

"Or what? You'll shoot me?" she said in a mocking tone. "How's your big fancy ritual going to work if I'm dead, huh?"

"I'm warning you..."

"And I'm telling you to do it! Pull the trigger, you fucking pussy!"

"Don't fucking tempt me!"

"Do it, motherfucker!"

Whether Bobby would have or not, Ava would never find out because in the next moment, the shack's door exploded in a cacophony of splintered wood as the Rider burst into the room. He stepped over the cabinet and stood in front of them, brandishing his machete, the same weapon that took Jeremy from her. His face remained uncovered, a rotting monument to that night all those years ago. His dead eyes locked on her and she couldn't look away, no matter how much she wanted to. Her timing would need to be perfect.

Bobby stood still in front of him. She couldn't quite see his butthole pucker, but his posture was stiff and nervous. His plan was about to backfire and he knew it.

"Caleb..."

The Rider tilted his head at the mention of his long forgotten name.

"I'm sorry, Caleb. I didn't see it back then, but I see it now. You needed to make the sacrifice."

The Rider righted his head as Bobby continued.

"See?" he said, gesturing toward Ava. "I got her for you. I tried to match the symbols, but had to take my time to make sure I got it right. Now that you're here, you can do it however you need to."

Ava dug her feet into the ground and tried to push back as hard as she could without making it obvious. The post shifted some more.

The Rider took a step forward and Bobby took one back. He pulled his gun and pointed it at his former friend.

"Don't come any closer," he said in a shaky voice. "I got you what you wanted. Take her and let me go."

Ava pushed back a little harder. This time the post obviously shook as the Rider looked past him, taking note of what she was trying to do.

He advanced again and Bobby pulled the trigger, the crack of the pistol reverberating through the tiny structure. The bullet found its home in the Rider's chest, but he didn't so much as flinch. Before Bobby could pull the trigger a second time, the Rider thrust his machete upward and through the bottom of his chin. Ava screamed as she saw the blade exit the top of his skull, a fresh coat of blood splattering her face.

It was time for the final push, figuratively and literally. While the Rider relished in ending the life of the man who had ended his, Ava used all her remaining strength to swing her legs up against Bobby's back, her feet landing directly on the grinning skull in the center of his vest. She pushed as hard as she could and thrust herself back, the post dislodging from the ground and sending her tumbling backward.

As the wooden pillar collapsed, it crashed through the rickety wall of the structure, sending it, and Ava, outside. As she hit the ground, the lower left side of her body flashed with a lightning bolt of agony. She wanted nothing more than to just lie there, to let the pain overtake her, for her consciousness to slip away yet again, but she thought of Jeremy and their baby. As the thought of her child entered her mind, so did a wave of panic. She looked down and saw a large, jagged piece of wood sticking out of her side. The baby! Was the baby okay? It looked like it was far enough off to the side, but she didn't know. She could only hope at this point.

She pushed herself up with every fiber of her being, the wood splintering off, sticking out of both her back and front. She'd seen enough medical shows to know not to try to extract it, otherwise she could bleed out before she had a chance to escape. As she got to her feet, she saw the Rider through the wreckage of the shack, Bobby's corpse slumped at his feet. For what felt like the thousandth time, she met his eyes, which were both knowing and soulless at the same time.

"Okay, motherfucker. Let's go."

Ava made a motion like she was going to charge forward and she saw the Rider step back ever so slightly in preparation, but instead, she pivoted and ran around the outside of the shack. She was once a track star, running coming as naturally as breathing, but years of "taking it easy" out of concern for health combined with the hell her body had been through made it feel like she was trekking through quicksand. As she rounded the front, the Rider was already emerging from the shattered doorframe. He lunged at her, but Ava found the strength to pick up her gait, causing him to just narrowly miss grabbing a handful of her hair. She kept running as she saw the red light of Bobby's flares in the distance. Her body ached and her lungs burned, but she kept moving, only stopping once to steal a glance behind her. The Rider was pursuing, but walking steadily and confidently. His nonchalant pace scared Ava. He was not worried about her getting away. And why would he be? She was broken and damaged, wounded prey ready to be put down.

But she thought of her parents. She thought of Jeremy. And she thought of their child. She had spent the start of her adult life not caring if she lived or died, but the only thing she wanted, more than anything in this moment, was to survive. She wanted to live so badly, it spurred her forward, allowing her to widen the gap between her and her pursuer.

She came to the end of the road where Bobby had parked the car and felt a rush of euphoria at seeing it was still there. She stumbled and hit the ground in front of the bumper, but scurried around the side on her hands and knees, yanking the door open as quickly as she could before shutting it just as fast. She slapped the lock closed and pushed down on the brake with her mangled right foot. It hurt like a son of a bitch, but she would be safe soon. She pressed the ignition button.

Nothing.

"Fuck!" she shouted as she remembered that there weren't any keys and that Bobby had hotwired it to start it, a technique she knew nothing about.

She tried to recall what he had done, looking at the wires dangling underneath the steering wheel. She grabbed two of them and tried to strike them together, hoping to spark the engine, but nothing.

"Goddamn it!" she cried in frustration.

She dropped the wires, knowing that it was hopeless, and tried to think of her next move, but she didn't have time.

The Rider's fist smashed through the window and this time, he managed to grab a clump of her hair, pulling her toward him.

"No!" she screamed as she tried to push herself in the opposite direction while grabbing for anything to stop her momentum toward him, her left hand clasping onto the rearview mirror which promptly broke off as the monster pulled her out of the car. As she felt her back scrape against the glass of the shattered window, she did the only thing she could think of. She turned the broken connector of the mirror and thrust it back wildly hoping to get lucky. She did.

The jagged metal impaled the Rider's left eye and he lost his grip in the shock. He stumbled backward, confused and trying to yank it out.

Ava ran around the car and saw another avenue to safety. The Rider's motorcycle.

She hadn't ridden one in a few years since she and her ex had broken up, and certainly not one like this, but she hoped it wouldn't be too different. She hopped on and started it, the thunderous sound hurting her ears as it roared to life. The handlebars were hot. Almost too hot to bear, but she held on nonetheless. Her life depended on it. She flicked on the light just in time to see the Rider snap the rearview mirror out of his eye, leaving a chunk inside, his face riddled with anger, the first emotion she'd seen from him. She backed up, getting ready to turn and head toward the highway, but something Bobby, of all people, said resonated with her.

"He isn't going to stop coming for you."

Where was she going to go? The hospital? A police station? This thing had already barreled through both of those supposedly safe havens without breaking a sweat. There was a military base on the way back north, but that was a good fifty miles away. No way she would make it that far.

An idea entered her mind. It was improbable and there was no guarantee it would work, but she had to try. She revved the engine and rode off into the trees, narrowly escaping the Rider as she did.

Chapter 21

Ava maneuvered the motorcycle with sheer willpower, barely missing crashing into trees on more than one occasion, but she kept her speed under control, following the markers Bobby had left behind until she saw the shack. She could see through the busted-open door all the way back into the woods through the hole in the back wall. She took the bike right up to the doorframe and quickly dismounted, her hands feeling like she'd just held a hot pan. She reached down and pushed the cabinet aside. It was heavy and her midsection burned around the wood jutting out of it, but it moved slowly out of the way.

When she had a wide-enough berth, she went back to the side of the motorcycle and gripped the handlebars on either side. Her hands were numb and adrenaline coursed through her, so the burning did not feel as severe the second time around. She rolled the bike into the shack and tipped it on its side next to Bobby's corpse. She looked down at his mangled face. An eyeball had popped out and rested on the ground next to him, still connected by the ocular nerve. Fucking coward.

She found the gas cap and popped it out. Even with her broken nose, Ava could still smell the stench of gasoline as it filled the shack. Thank goodness there were enough holes in the structure—some new, some old—to ventilate it a bit or she might very easily pass out. And she knew that would be the end of her.

"Fight, Ava," Jeremy's voice came from some ethereal location. "Just a bit longer."

She didn't know if it was a hallucination or if he had become her personal Obi Wan, but it didn't matter. He was right. She had to finish this. Just one last push.

Ava grabbed the gun that rested next to the body. After that she rolled him over and rummaged through his pockets, fishing out the tattered ritual page. As she pulled it out, her hand brushed against a small metal object. A lighter. Finally, something going right.

Her joy was short-lived as she looked up to see the Rider standing in the doorway. She quickly rose to her feet, pain racking her body as she stared him down, looking him right in his remaining eye. She smiled and held up the page.

"Is this what you want, Caleb?"

He took a step forward but she flicked the lighter open and ignited the flame, holding it mere millimeters from the fragile paper.

"Uh uh, you son of a bitch."

He stopped.

"I don't know what this is all about. I don't know who this master is that you serve, but I don't fucking care. This ends now."

His lip curled into a sneer, rage boiling him from the inside as Ava taunted him. The reaction told her what she needed to know. This page was important.

"I'm not Vicki. I'm not your sacrifice. And if I burn this, you will never be free of your debt."

His fist clenched. Ava took a step back. The Rider took another step forward. She moved the lighter closer, singeing the edge. He stopped again. She took another step back and felt her heel brush against the wood just below the hole she had made her first exit through. She had gone far enough. The toe on her opposite foot felt wet all of a sudden. She glanced down to see that the gasoline trail had reached the end of the shack. She sidestepped out of its path.

"I'm going to leave now, Caleb. And you're going to stay right fucking there. If I so much as sense you following me, I will burn this and you will be damned forever."

The Rider remained silent and motionless.

"I'll take the fact that you're not moving as meaning you understand me. Do you understand me, Caleb?"

Still nothing. She was using his living name to throw him off and it seemed like it was working.

Ava lifted one leg and carefully stepped over the bottom of the hole. "Oh, and Caleb?"

He tilted his head again, looking for her follow-up.

"Fuck you."

She brought the lighter up to the paper. It caught quickly, the flame licking her hand as she dropped it right in the puddle of gasoline.

A rope of flame slithered along the ground to the bike. When it made contact, the shack erupted in a ball of flame and, for the first time, the Rider screamed, an unearthly howl that rattled the trees along with the explosion. Ava was thrown back and hit the ground hard again. She writhed for a moment, trying to compose herself until she managed to prop up on her elbows. Her eyes bulged as she saw the Rider, or what had to be him, completely engulfed in flames and walking through the burning structure toward her. She fell back down and looked up at the lone star she saw in the night sky as she started to cry.

"Jeremy. I'm sorry. I tried. I love you."

As she waited for the fire-coated monster to take her away, she heard a loud crack ahead. She pushed herself back up just in time to see the roof completely collapse, a beam smashing right into the Rider's skull, sending him crashing to the ground. She held herself up for as long as she could, terrified that he would rise again, but he didn't. Ava used the rest of her strength to get herself into a seated position. She used her hands to scoot back toward the nearest pine tree. When she felt the bark on her back, she pushed herself against it and sat, pulling her legs up against her chest.

She sat and cried and watched the Rider burn.

Epilogue

Ava sat on the exam table and ran her fingers across the freshly healed incision below her left shoulder blade. It didn't hurt anymore, but it felt a little odd to the touch, but she guessed that was just what scars were. She had certainly amassed enough of them during her ordeal eighteen months ago. What was one more?

Her thoughts were interrupted by a quick knock followed by the door opening. She smiled politely at Dr. Carabelli as he entered the room.

"Ava," he said. "How are you feeling?"

That felt like a strange question. She'd felt a lot since she and Jeremy had left that hotel. There was pain and grief. Plenty of it. But there was also joy, purpose and resolve. To say it was a roller coaster of a year and a half would be an understatement.

That final night of terror, Ava had fallen asleep against the tree as the shack burned. When she'd woken up, it was in a hospital several days later. She would eventually be told that the doctors had kept her sedated as to not put too much strain on her heart. Her first reaction was panic, but the doctors had sedated her again. When she came to again, the police were there. The first thing they did was confirm what she already knew. Jeremy was dead. The pain hit her again like a tidal wave and she cried for a long time. They also told her there were two bodies found in the wreckage. The first had been identified through dental records as Robert Fletcher, a member of a notorious biker gang that had supposedly disbanded years ago. They had been suspects in an arms deal that had gone bad, but they were never able to pin the crime on any of them and any remaining members had seemingly been off the grid ever since. The other they couldn't identify, but they confirmed that he was indeed very dead. When she asked what they did with the body, they told her they would hold it for thirty days and, if unclaimed, it would be buried in the potter's field with the other unidentified bodies found over the years.

Her recovery was slow. When her parents were finally permitted to come in and see her, they were relieved to see that she was alive, devastated about Jeremy and shocked at her pregnancy. Momma and Poppa held her tight and the three of them cried for a long time. The doctors confirmed that, miraculously, the baby had been unharmed throughout the traumatic events she had suffered, but they were concerned about her ability to carry it to term due to her ARVD, which had been exacerbated by the trauma.

"I'm going to have this baby," she stated defiantly.

The doctors told her that she would have to be extremely careful and mostly on bed rest. Ava agreed and decided to forego her traditional flippancy in regard to her health. She left the hospital after a week and returned north with her parents. She let them fuss over and help her as much as they wanted. Even when she felt those old twinges of rebellion.

The only time she left the house was for doctors' appointments and for Jeremy's funeral. His body had been recovered and sent home. His father, sanctimonious dickhead that he was, threw a lavish funeral and put on his best sad face for his ass-kissing social circle. He was cordial to Ava who sat by the coffin the entire wake, marveling at how well the funeral home had preserved him. He truly looked like he was resting. She didn't tell his dad about the pregnancy and made sure her parents didn't slip up and say anything either. As far as she was concerned, once Jeremy was buried, there was no reason to ever see Andrew Carlisle again, a feeling that she was sure was mutual.

After the funeral, she called the county every day to see if someone had claimed Caleb Anders's body. She didn't say it on the phone, but her actual intention was to make sure that his body was still there. She'd had more than a few nightmares of the Rider pulling up outside her house and killing her family before cutting the baby from her stomach. The dreams often ended with the Rider driving away with her baby while she crawled futilely after them. As the motorcycle faded away in the distance, she would wake up screaming and drenched in sweat.

Finally, when she called on an otherwise nondescript Tuesday afternoon, the woman on the line confirmed that the John Doe found in the pines last month had been buried. She wasn't completely satisfied with that. She would have much preferred that they cremated him, and had made that known with just about every inquiry, but this would have to do. It was over.

She had to believe it really was over.

When her pregnancy entered month five, she went for her standard ultrasound. The doctor confirmed that everything looked good and that the baby was healthy.

They asked if she wanted to know the sex. She did, but she paused. An unsettling thought popped into her head. What if it was a girl? One that looked just like her, which would mean she looked just like Vicki. Would that trigger the nightmare anew? Or if it was a boy, would it look like Jeremy? Would she feel his loss over and over every time she looked at him?

These thoughts raced through her head, each scenario bringing joy and terror in equal measure. As she contemplated, she looked over in the corner and, for a split second, saw Jeremy sitting in a chair in the corner of the room behind the ultrasound machine. He looked just like she remembered him the morning they checked out of the hotel, dressed in his shorts and favorite shirt. He beamed that winning smile at her and winked before he was gone as quickly as he appeared.

She took a deep breath and pushed all the negative thoughts out of her head. She resolved that their baby was a blessing and, while there would certainly be ups and downs, especially raising it by herself, she would fight every day to ensure that this child would never know horror like its mom and dad experienced.

"Tell me."

A little more than seven months after the nightmare ended, her parents drove her to the hospital for her scheduled C-section. Her cardiologist insisted that if she was going to have the baby, this was the way it had to be. The operating table felt cold underneath her as they gave her the epidural. She was nervous and wanted Jeremy to be there more than anything, but Mama stayed with her and held her hand, talking to her the whole time, soothing her in the way that only a mother can. She didn't feel a thing as they cut into her, adding another scar to her collection; instead, she felt an eerie sense of calm wash over her. When she heard her son cry for the first time, she was overwhelmed with happiness. He cooed as they handed him to her and she brushed the fine tuft of blond hair on his head.

"Hi, Jeremy. Mommy loves you so much."

Once she'd recovered from the C-section and had time to bond and care for baby Jeremy those first few months, it was time to deal with one more procedure. She never intended to do it, but now that she was responsible for this little child that she loved more than she ever thought possible, she knew she finally needed to be serious about her health, so she agreed to have a defibrillator put in. On the day of the procedure, she once again found herself being wheeled into an operating room, only this time Mama wasn't with her. She knew she had to go at this one alone. As the anesthesiologist placed the mask over her face and started the intravenous drip, he asked her to count back from one hundred. When she got to ninety-eight, she saw Jeremy once again standing over the doctor's shoulder. He winked at her and mouthed the words "You got this." She counted down to ninety-six and was out.

When she woke up in recovery, the nurse told her how well she did and that the doctor would be in to see her shortly, but she wasn't listening. She scanned the room, looking to see if Jeremy was still there, but he wasn't. Her eyes watered and she closed them tight before the tears could escape, knowing in her heart that she had seen him for the last time.

It had now been three weeks since she came home from the hospital and she was here for a follow-up with Dr. C, as his patients affectionately referred to him. He was personable and handsome and, if Ava had any interest in dating, he might have even been her type, but she was still grieving her husband while focusing on being a mom. She was just thankful that he was the best cardiac surgeon on the east coast. His role was to give her a shot at the best quality of life she could have given her circumstances.

"I'm feeling okay," she told him, having almost forgotten the question as she recounted the events that brought her here.

He pulled her gown down off her shoulder slightly so he could examine the scar.

"It's healing nicely."

"Good to hear."

They talked for a bit. He asked how the baby was and she told him he was amazing. He reiterated that this procedure was the best thing for her and would ensure that she would be around for a long time for her child. She asked about her physical limitations and he told her light exercise was fine, and that she should just pay attention to her heart rate. But he urged her to ease into it so as not to put too much stress on her heart too quickly. She thanked him and left. Papa was in the lobby, waiting to drive her home. He stood up as she walked out and put an arm around her, hugging her close.

"All good?" he asked.

"All good, Papa."

Ava went straight to the nursery when she got home. Little Jeremy was asleep in his crib, looking angelic lying there with what she liked to refer to as "grumpy baby face," his tiny features almost looking annoyed as he slept. She could already see so much of his father in him that it made her soul happy and hurt at the same time. She missed him so much and was so grateful to have this piece of him to carry with her forever. She always felt like she could never love anyone as much as she did her late husband, but this little miracle in front of her threw that theory out the window. She only prayed that he would never experience anything even remotely as horrific as his parents had. She wondered what she would tell him when he asked how his father died. Would she tell him the truth? Or just a version of it? She wanted him to know that he died saving her life, but if she could spare him the details, she would, even though she valued honesty above all else. Whatever she decided, at least she didn't have to do that right now.

Baby Jeremy opened his eyes and smiled at her. He was such a good baby. He ate well. He slept well. Ava often found herself in disbelief at just how good he was. She lifted him out of his crib and cradled him close, kissing his chubby cheeks and eliciting a giggle. She looked at the clock in the corner of the room.

"You must be getting hungry."

He squealed with delight.

"Let's get you something to eat."

She carried him downstairs. Mama and Papa were sitting on the couch, watching some old black-and-white movie that Ava didn't immediately recognize. Mama heard them and turned her head and smiled. She pointed at the TV.

"Ava Gardner. Great movie."

Ava returned her smile and retrieved a bottle of formula from the fridge. She heated it up and tested it on her arm to make sure it wasn't too hot. She turned to go back upstairs.

"Tell Nonna and Nonno we'll see them soon."

Jeremy cooed again and her parents smiled as they went back upstairs.

Ava went back into Jeremy's room and settled into the rocking chair into the corner. Jeremy eagerly accepted the bottle and started chugging it down as Ava lay back and closed her eyes. She sat contentedly until she heard a sound that made her blood run cold.

She opened her eyes wide and felt her heartbeat quicken.

A single tear streamed down her face as the sound of the motorcycle grew louder.

Afterword

Wow. We made it to the end. This book was a long time coming. Ten plus years in fact. I had the idea while driving back from Atlantic City on Route 539 one Sunday afternoon. A guy on a motorcycle dressed all in black with a helmet fully obscuring his face followed me for a good fifteen miles or so. I'm sure he was perfectly nice and had no ill intentions, but it was definitely a little unsettling and the seed of a story was planted.

Over the years there have been many starts and stops. I worked on multiple drafts as a short story, a screenplay and, ultimately, what became the novel you just finished. I changed the setting from Las Vegas to Atlantic City (why it didn't occur to me to set it in A.C. initially is beyond me given its genesis) and I updated the original ending which had Jeremy and the Rider getting washed away in a flash flood. For all the starts and stops and trepidation that came with producing this work, I'm very happy with how the story turned out and, more importantly, I hope you are too!

Sooooo, if you did enjoy this twisted little tale, I'd ask that you kindly leave a review on Amazon, Barnes and Noble or wherever else you may have purchased this book. Your support means the world and will help me craft more terrifying tales for your enjoyment!

Also, please come hang out with me on my website - www.jameskaine.net! There you can sign up for my **VIP Readers Club** and get a 100% free eBook. You'll also be the first to know about my upcoming projects as well as contests and giveaways. You can also follow me on social media if you are so inclined via the links on my site.

I know your time is valuable and there are literally millions of books you could have chosen, so I can't thank you enough for choosing mine! I can't wait for you to see what's coming up in the future!

Until next time, my friends.

-James Kaine

About Author

James Kaine specializes in gritty, no holds barred horror. A true student of the genre, he writes characters you can care about...and then subjects them to horrors beyond your imagination.

Despite all that, James is a pretty nice guy. A New Jersey native, he still resides there with his wife, two children and his loyal Boston Terrier. Aside from writing, he enjoys movies, music and trying to play guitar. He is a die-hard New York Giants fan, which, in recent years, has been more horrifying than anything he could put on paper.

Sign up for the James Kaine VIP Readers Club at www.jameskaine.net and get a free eBook!

JAMES KAINE

Follow James on Social Media:

Facebook – JamesKaineWrites

Twitter - @JamesKaineBooks

Instagram - @JamesKaineWrites

Printed in Great Britain
by Amazon

40883153R00158